EXPLORING MUSIC THROUGH EXPERIENCE

Second Edition

Joseph E. Koob II

UNIVERSITY
PRESS OF
AMERICA

LANHAM • NEW YORK • LONDON

Copyright © 1984 by

University Press of America,™ Inc.

4720 Boston Way
Lanham, MD 20706

3 Henrietta Street
London WC2E 8LU England

Library of Congress Cataloging in Publication Data

Koob, Joseph E.
    Exploring music through experience.

    Bibliography: p.
    1. Music appreciation. I. Title.
MT90.K84   1984   780'.1'5   83–19864
ISBN 0–8191–3640–9 (alk. paper)
ISBN 0–8191–3641–7 (pbk. : alk. paper)

FOR MY WIFE

iv

I would like to acknowledge the following individuals for their inspiration and assistance with this work: Dr. Charles Leonhard, University of Illinois; Dr. Wilmer Kirschenmann, Northern State College; Dr. Theodora J. Koob; Katherine R. Koob; Nina Monahan; Vicki Reuer; and Mary Heidenreich.

I would also like to acknowledge a debt in this work to Donald Grout's, <u>A History of Western Music</u>, with which I have been familiar for over fifteen years and presently have the pleasure of using in teaching my classes.

Special thanks to my Mother, Theodora J. Koob, for her assistance in preparing both editions.

TABLE OF CONTENTS

PREFACE

This work was conceived as a practicable alternative to the current genre of Music Appreciation texts. Its main purpose is to give non-music students the background needed to understand HOW MUSIC WORKS. The text, while following the traditional major sections of music fundamentals and music history, emphasizes the RELATIONAL aspects of the elements of music and also offers a broad, general approach to the development of Western music history as a basis for better understanding of the music we come into contact with every day.

This author feels that there is a need for an abbreviated Music Appreciation text that allows the teacher flexibility to choose his/her own materials for listening and analysis. The emphasis away from the detailed historical and analytic approach and toward the relational concepts of music fundamentals will give the instructor freedom to lecture within his/her interests and experiences and not be tied down to the choices and interests of the author.

More emphasis is placed on HOW the system works than on having students manipulate various elements within the system. This results in an approach that introduces the elements of music in a very fundamental, easily understandable manner with the history of music a broad expansion and progression of basic music concepts.

This work provides students with considerable background material for classroom and concert experiences. All music and musical learning should provide expressive experiences; therefore this text has been written as a foundation for increasing students' aesthetic experiences.

x

INTRODUCTION

In approaching this text the student should keep in mind that music, on every level, is an experience; thus, the discussion and analysis of various aspects and concepts of music must always refer back to the experience of music itself. The study of music fundamentals as a relational system plus a broad conception of the development of music history offers the student a basis for understanding classical music as well as whatever types of music he enjoys from day to day.

The music fundamentals section deals with a detailed introduction to the elements of music. This relational analysis, coupled with his classroom experiences, can give the student a firm basis in HOW music is put together, as well as the foundation for developing listening skills, beginning analysis, and further understanding.

The music history section follows two major musical concepts as the basis for understanding the continuity of Western musical development: texture--monophonic to polyphonic to homophonic and tonal systems-- modality to major-minor tonality to contemporary tonality and atonality. The emphasis is toward a broad understanding of major musical periods and their importance in the development of Western music.

The student is encouraged to take an active part in musical experiences. Only through exposure to the creative and expressive qualities of music will the serious student truly understand and appreciate a wide variety of music. Aesthetic enjoyment and active listening should be the primary goals in Music Appreciation.

PART I

The Elements of Music

Everyone comes into contact with music everyday
and much of the time it is simply taken for granted.
The inundation of sound that bombards our senses from
multiple sources is often entirely ignored or barely
noticed by our conscious minds. With the amount of music
available today, it is amazing how few people have even
a basic understanding of what music is and how it is
created; in other words, an understanding of what is
sometimes referred to as the fundamentals of music.

Primarily the music we hear is expressive; that is
its main purpose. However, in order to discuss music in
this text it is necessary to deal with the abstract
elements that we use to portray music: <u>pitch</u>-- the
highness or lowness of sound; <u>duration</u>-- which includes
beat or pulse, rhythm, meter, motion, <u>et cetera</u>;
<u>dynamics</u>-- the intensity of the sound; and <u>timbre</u>-- the
tone color or quality. To have a beginning understanding
of music the student needs to relate these elements to
listening, creation, and participation in the expressive
qualities of music. The first four chapters of this text
will discuss in detail how these four elements are formed and used in our present musical language.

In addition to pitch, duration, dynamics, and
timbre a general overview of several other aspects of
music will also be presented: aspects that include some
or all of the "basic four ingredients of music" studied
in the first four chapters; chapter five will cover the
topics of melody and harmony: tonality, keys, chords,
<u>et cetera</u>; chapter six: musical organization, or form,
texture, and style; chapter seven: attending recitals
of classical music.**

**The term <u>classical</u> in reference to music is used in
two distinct ways. Here it means serious music of
Western Culture. There is also a <u>Classical</u> period
(1750-1825) and Classical music would then refer to a
specific style of music composed during that period of
time. As both words are used in musical terminology
interchangeably, this book will make no attempt to
change that usage; however, reference to the Classical
period will be capitalized and reference to <u>c</u>lassical
or serious music will not be capitalized.

To the non-music student the "foreign language" of music sometimes seems barely approachable it its celestial sphere. But as you will soon see music is largely a relational system and in many of its basic elements it is much more easily understandable than foreign languages or complex mathematics. Part of that understanding is simple awareness, and another important addition to learning about music is experience and participation. For all that you may read and listen, true understanding comes from involvement in the processes of musical performance.

It is very important to remember as you progress in your understanding of music that the primary purpose of music is expressive in nature. Understanding some of the general aspects of music should add to your appreciation of the expressive function of music whether it is classical music or jazz, folk, or rock and roll. If you approach the study of this book with this key idea in mind you will hopefully gain some insights into the music you do appreciate as part of your everyday lives.

Chapter I

Pitch

Pitch in music can be defined as the highness or lowness of sound.

Scientifically, pitch is directly related to the number of vibrations per second emitted by a vibrating object, transmitted through the air to our ears, and then experienced in our brain as a particular sound or tone. Any of a wide variety of objects can be set into vibration to produce sound audible to our ears and the characteristics of the particular object will affect the pitch of the sound or the number of vibrations per second.

The faster the number of vibrations per second of a sounding body the higher the pitch will be; the slower the vibrations per second the lower the pitch.

For example: W————————————————X
                Δ   Δ

If a string (line WX) is stretched between two points (W and X) and anchored at those points, when it is set in motion (as in plucking a guitar string), it will vibrate at some pitch or at a specific number of vibrations per second depending on several important factors: the tension of the string and the thickness and length. If we change any of these factors affecting the vibrating body, in this case the string WX, the pitch of the sound emitted from the string will change.

If the string is lengthened the pitch will be lower, assuming that all the other factors remain the same. And if it is shortened the pitch will rise. Also the larger or thicker the string the lower the pitch and vice versa.

Increased tension will make the string vibrate more quickly and thus the pitch will rise; decreased tension will lower the pitch.

These factors affecting the pitch of a vibrating string will also affect any vibrating body in the same manner. Size (length of tubing, thickness, general size of the vibrating body)-- the larger the size the lower the pitch, and tension (lip tension, tightness of the drum head, <u>et cetera</u>)-- the more tension the higher the pitch, will affect the pitch.

Another factor that concerns the scientist and the musician in relation to pitch is temperature. However for our discussion we will assume that the vibrating body will remain at a constant temperature.

We will return to the string diagram in a moment to illustrate another aspect of musical pitch, but first let us take up the discussion of the symbols used in our musical language: notation.

The symbols used in music to designate pitch are called "<u>notes</u>."

Notes: o   d ♩ ♭

All of you are familiar with what notes look like but you may not "read" music or understand the <u>relational</u> system that is used to indicate pitch in music. While it is not the purpose of this text or of the course to teach you to read music fluently, we hope to give you a basic comprehension of this system, how it evolved, and how it works.

To <u>verbally</u> symbolize pitch we use the first seven letters of our alphabet: A B C D E F G. If we need to go higher or lower we simply "re-use" the letters: higher than G would be:

A B C D E F G⌐A B C D <u>et</u> <u>cetera</u>
   ⌐_____→

(See page 12 for a diagram of the piano keyboard to help illustrate this concept.)

Lower than A would be:

<u>et</u> <u>cetera</u> E F G⌐A B C D E F G
           ←_____⌐

When we repeat the letter name of a note, i.e. an "A" and a higher "A" we are dealing with an important scientific musical principle. Two notes of the same name, one of higher pitch than another ("A" and another "A") sound somehow similar to us. The reason that this is true is because one of the pitches is exactly twice the number of vibrations per second as the other. This would also be true of two "C's", two "D's", <u>et</u> <u>cetera</u>.

4

We call this distance between two notes of the same name an octave, from the Latin word for eight--both being eight tones apart (if you count the tone you start on and the tone you end on).

```
A B C D E F G A
1 2 3 4 5 6 7 8
```

One of the tones is exactly double the number of vibrations per second of the other.

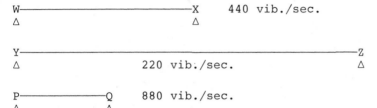

W————————————————————X   440 vib./sec.
Δ   Δ

Y——————————————————————————————————————Z
Δ   220 vib./sec.   Δ

P——————————Q   880 vib./sec.
Δ   Δ

Returning to string WX you can see that with all other factors remaining constant, a string twice as long, YZ, will vibrate at half the frequency (vibrations per second) of string WX, and a string twice as short, PQ, will vibrate twice as fast. Each pitch in our system would be designated as an "A": the "A" of string PQ sounding one octave above the string WX and two octaves above string YZ.

Further, if an obstruction (a finger will do nicely) is placed in the middle of string YZ and then either side of the string is plucked, the tones will sound exactly one octave higher than the string YZ plucked without being stopped. This is one fundamental way that different pitches are produced on most instruments: the length of the vibrating body is chang-.ed.

The octave is the most important interval (the distance between two pitches or notes) in all music. Most musical systems use the octave as a basic building block and divide it into smaller units. Our particular "Western" (referring generally to European music history and presently including the Americas) system is unique because of HOW we divide the octave up into smaller intervals. This will be discussed shortly.

To make music comprehensible to the performer and easier to read, we set the notes on a relational grid.

5

A series of five equidistant parallel lines is used, resulting in "five lines and four spaces" as the grid for distinquishing between specific pitches. This is called a musical staff.

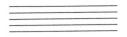

The staff by itself simply indicates the relative highness or lowness of pitch (up the staff the pitch is higher, down the staff, lower).

Higher--up   Lower--down

It is necessary to further specify an absolute pitch to fit the staff and relate the other notes to it. A clef is added to the staff to orient the staff to a specific note. A clef can be defined as a device that is placed at the beginning of a staff to designate a specific relational tone. For instance, a common clef used today is the treble or "G" clef.

△ note G

This clef "circles" the second line from the bottom of the staff (indicated by the arrow to the side of the staff) and indicates that this line will represent the pitch "G" (approximately 392 vibrations/second). Once this pitch has been established, all the other notes on the staff will be related to this pitch. By adding notes on each line and space on either side of this set pitch we can quickly relate the other pitch names to the given pitch.

D E F G A B C D E F G

Since we use more pitches than this staff can accomodate, we can add extra lines to the top or bottom of the staff in order to read notes above or below the staff. These lines are called <u>ledger</u> (leger) lines. (Both spellings are correct.)

Often however, to avoid extensive use of ledger lines, composers will use other clefs.

The second most common clef is called the bass clef or "F" clef.

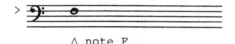

△ note F

It is used with lower sounding (bass) instruments like cellos, tubas, <u>et cetera</u>. (The treble clef is used with higher, treble instruments like violins, flutes, <u>et cetera</u>.)

With the bass clef at the beginning of the staff the two dots of the clef "surround" the second line from the top of the staff and indicate the pitch "F" (approximately 174 vibrations per second--over one octave below the "G" of the treble clef.)

This clef greatly extends the range of our musical language and on the piano, which has a very wide range, the treble and bass clefs are used together, creating the <u>Grand Staff</u>.

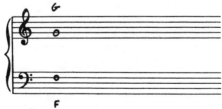

Thus the pianist must read two different "languages" or relational systems at the same time.

7

As you can see if a ledger line is used between the treble and bass clefs the clefs will, in fact, meet and overlap. The note where the two staffs meet is called "middle C".

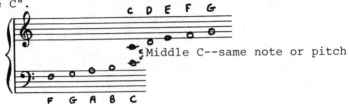

Middle C--same note or pitch

It should also be noted that it is possible to designate all the different pitches on the staffs by letter names and numbers separating one octave from another.

As indicated, the middle octave is designated C D E F G A B and the lower octaves have numbers to the right and lower than the letter pitch designation, i.e. "C_1". The upper octaves have the number to the right and slightly above the pitch letter, i.e. "C^1". Occasionally the upper octaves may be further indicated by use of a lower case letter, i.e. "c^1". The number differentiates how many octaves a pitch is above or below the middle octave. A "C_2" would indicate the pitch two octaves below middle "C".

A third clef is standardly used in music.

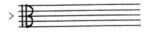

This clef, called the "C" clef or movable "C" clef, designates the pitch "middle C" (approximately 216 vibrations per second). It can be moved to different positions on the staff if desired, each position always indicating the placement of the pitch "middle C".

(all indicate the same pitch of 216 vibrations/second)
Each position sets up a different absolute reference
point for musical pitch on the staff.

This staff is used for medium range instruments,
the viola being the most common.

viola clef

Sometimes it is used to avoid ledger lines when a part
written for a lower instrument extends for a long period
of time above the bass clef.

cello

in bass clef

with a change to moveable "C" clef.

cello

section remains
on staff in "C"
clef

Once some relational system has been set up on a
staff, figuring out the pitches in a piece of music is
fairly easy. It does take considerable practice to gain
facility in reading music at a fast speed, but the
system itself is very basic. Something that is more
difficult to comprehend is the Western scale system.

From our earlier discussion of the octave you
became acquainted briefly with the term interval. An
interval in music is the distance between two notes.
The distance between two consecutive notes in our
musical language is called a step (or an interval of a

9

second [see page 17 for further discussion of inter-vals]), i.e. C to D.

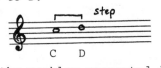

However, the problem presented in our scale system is that the steps are not equidistant! The distance between tones in our octave, i.e. C D E F G A B C, is not constant. (A <u>scale</u> can be defined simply as an arrangement of pitches from highest to lowest or lowest to highest.)

For many, many years of music history the music sung was improvised from short motives (melodies or tunes) that, when finally formed into a system of scales, utilized a series of eight tones to form the scale within an octave. Though consecutive letter names were used for the notes, each of these scales was built on an irregular pattern of intervals (steps) within the octave. For the past several hundred years our octave has been divided into twelve equal "half-steps" formed by thirteen pitches (see chromatic scale below, page 11). But since our scales are derived from past musical heritage, they are built using only eight of the possible thirteen tones comprising the octave, pre-serving irregular interval patterns in our common scales.

If we map out the distances between notes in the octave C to C^1 you will see that "half-steps" occur only between the third and fourth notes and the seventh and eighth notes. The other intervals are "whole-steps", equal to two "half-steps".

whole step symbol: ⌐   half step symbol: ∧

Octave C to C^1:

or:

(It may be helpful to look at the piano keyboard. See page 12 for a diagram of the piano keyboard. The "white keys" represent the notes C D E F G A B C; the "black keys" represent the half steps inbetween the whole steps.)

If you total the whole and half steps between the octave C to C¹ you will find five whole steps (equal to ten half steps) and two half steps, or totaled together, twelve half steps.

The other half step intervals capable within the octave C to C¹ are designated by adding symbols called accidentals to the existing note names. These accidentals will affect the note or pitch in a specific way. The sharp (#) will raise the pitch of the note one half step, i.e. C to C# (C sharp), which will then be a note halfway between C and D. A flat sign (b) will lower the pitch of a note one half step, i.e. Bb (B flat), which will then be a note halfway between A and B. The natural sign (♮) will return a previously altered (raised or lowered) note back to its "regular" or "natural" pitch, i.e. a C# with a natural in front of it would become a C, and a Bb with a natural would become a B:

Here is a diagram of the twelve half steps of the octave and their names. As you can see, by using either sharps or flats notes may have the same pitch but a different name. These are called enharmonic notes, i.e. C# and Db.

Looking at the piano keyboard you will notice that the white keys C to C¹ form the pattern of whole steps seen in the scale C D E F G A B C¹, and that the black keys form the "missing" half steps. (see next page)

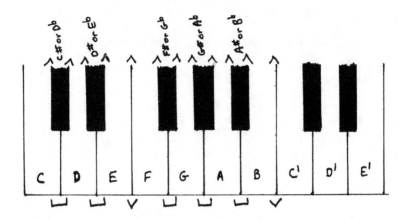

The pattern formed by the notes C D E F G A B C^1 is the <u>major</u> scale pattern: whole step, whole step, half step, whole step, whole step, whole step, half step-- equal to twelve half steps.

In <u>C major</u> the note "C" is the tonal center of the scale and is called the "<u>tonic</u>" or I (Roman numeral one) position of the scale.

In order to form <u>any</u> major scale the order of whole and half steps must be <u>preserved</u> regardless of what note you start on (or which note is the <u>tonic</u>): to demonstrate this principle we will use an illustration of half steps represented by circles. If you are familiar with the piano keyboard you may refer to the diagram above for this discussion.

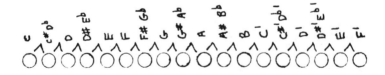

Sometimes it is difficult for the person with little or no keyboard experience to relate to the piano.

The above diagram should help you to understand the relationships of whole steps and half steps in a major scale as you see them developed below using the appropriate major scale pattern.

The distance between each note (circle) above is one half step. In order to form a major scale, regardless of what pitch it is started on, you will have to form the major scale pattern of whole steps and half steps: ws, ws, hs, ws, ws, ws, hs or the pattern of the notes C D E F G A B C[1], which as you have already seen fits this pattern. This is the C major scale, i.e. a scale built on the note C with the appropriate pattern of whole steps and half steps. The C major scale is illustrated below by filling in the circles that conform to the major pattern starting with the note C.

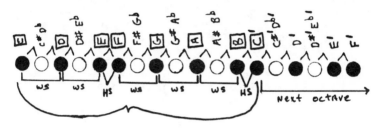

C major scale, Key of C major

However, if we want to form a D major scale (tonic or tonal center D) the notes D E F G A B C[1]D[1] will not give us the major scale pattern of ws, ws, hs, ws, ws, ws, hs; but the pattern ws, hs, ws, ws, ws, hs, ws.

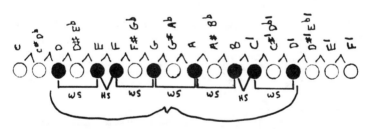

NOT a major scale pattern

So it is necessary to use other notes to form the correct pattern. We do this by using sharps or flats, depending on the order of the notes. (Always use consecutive letter names when forming a major scale

13

pattern, i.e. A, B, C, not A, A#, it would be correct
to use A, Bb in this circumstance.)

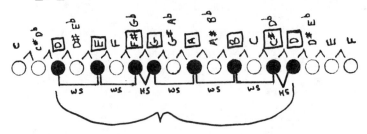

D major scale, Key of D major
notes: D E F# G A B C# D

In the case of D major the interval between E and
F is a half step, which will not fit the correct pattern
for a D major scale and so we raise the F to F# to
correct the problem. The same procedure is used for the
C to C#. Then to form a correct major scale on D it is
necessary to raise or sharp two of the tones, F and C,
a half step, to F# and C# respectively, to form the
correct pattern of whole steps and half steps.

To indicate to a performer that a piece is to be
played in a particular key, and that he should play
sharps on certain notes, the notes to be sharped (or
altered) are indicated at the front of the staff at the
right of the clef sign. This placement of accidentals,
called the key signature, indicates the key of the piece
by the number and type (sharps or flats--they are never
mixed) of accidentals being used. The key of C major
has no sharps or flats, and thus no key signature.

D major has two sharps, placed on the staff like
this:

If there are accidentals in a key signature the
performer is required to play all the pitches in the
piece represented in the key signature as sharps or
flats, regardless of the octave they appear in. Thus,
the example on the left (next page) is how it would
appear in the music, and the example on the right is
how it would be played.

14

written:  played:

Let us look at one more example of the formation of a major scale, this time in a "flat" key--a key using flats instead of sharps. If we start a scale on the note F as the tonic, using the same method we used for the D major scale, the notes F G A B C^1 D^1 E^1 F^1 do not fit the major scale pattern and consequently some alteration is needed.

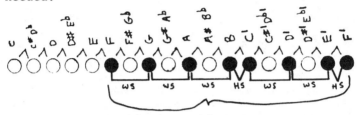

NOT a major scale pattern

Here the interval of a whole step between A and B is too large since it should be a half step, so it is necessary to lower the B by a half step by adding a flat: F G A Bb C^1 D^1 E^1 F^1. Then the pattern will be correct as seen below.

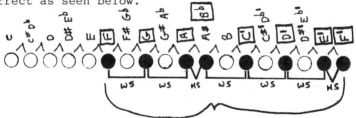

F major scale, Key of F major

Below is the key signature of F major.

You may want to try forming scales using the keyboard on page 12 as a guide. It is important to remember though to use all of the black keys as well as the white in considering half and whole steps. Once a person is familiar with the piano keyboard it is a handy reference for associating half and whole steps.

If you followed the process above you could easily

15

figure out all the different keys of the major scales by starting on different notes and establishing the number of accidentals needed to form the correct pattern. If you are interested in this, you should try it on both types of diagrams: circles and piano keyboard.

The major scales are not the only scales that we use in music. We also use three types of minor scales and other scales that use only five or six notes within the octave. Each of these scales sets up a set pattern of intervals (breaking up the twelve half steps differently) to form their particular scale and sound. Each of these different types of scales can also start on different notes (tonics), or in different keys, as long as their pattern of intervals remains the same.

It is not so important that you know the different patterns used in different scales, major and minor (for instance, the pure form of the minor is: ws, hs, ws, ws, hs, ws,ws), but it is important to understand the use of patterns and how they form scales, because it is the patterns of sounds of a particular scale that you relate and react to in the music to which you are listening. You are so used to hearing certain patterns (major and minor scales) that if they were changed in any way your ears would be very quick to tell you that something is different about the music. The major/minor tonal system has the ability to move you so strongly emotionally because of the expressive significance placed on the whole and half steps we just spent so much time discussing. This concept will be discussed in more detail in the chapter on melody and harmony.

The reason music from other cultures often sounds strange to us is because they use different scale patterns and even completely different divisions of the octave (not our twelve equal half steps). Some modern classical music sounds "weird" because of the wide variety of scales and patterns that are used which you are not accustomed to hearing.

There is one other scale that you should be familiar with, at least as far as terminology is concerned. The chromatic scale utilizes all twelve half steps in the octave: C C# D D# E F F# G G# A A# B C^1 (this has been diagrammed on page 11). In music the term chromatics or chromaticism refers to movement in half steps.

16

Intervals

Intervals (the distance between notes) are relatively easy to identify in music. You can either count from one note to another (i.e. C to G is the interval of a fifth: C D E F G--five notes; or C to F a fourth: C D E F--four notes), or accomplish the same principle on the staff by counting the lines and spaces between notes. In using either method BE SURE to count the note (line or space) you start on and end on.

Intervals:

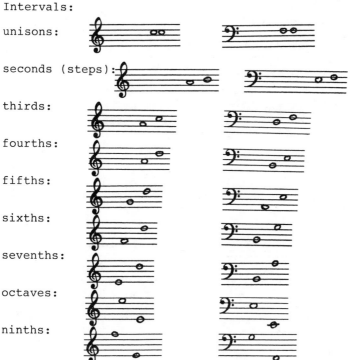

unisons:

seconds (steps):

thirds:

fourths:

fifths:

sixths:

sevenths:

octaves:

ninths:

(Intervals can be of any width: tenths, elevenths, et cetera.)

For the musician intervals are further specified by their exact nature. Thus we have perfect, major, minor, diminished, and augmented intervals, i.e. a major third is equal to two steps (C to E) and a minor third is equal to a step and a half (C to E-flat).

17

Chapter I: Glossary

<u>pitch</u>: highness or lowness of sound

<u>duration</u>: time elements of music including beat, rhythm, and motion

<u>dynamics</u>: intensity or loudness of sound

<u>timbre</u>: tone color or quality of sound

<u>classical music</u>: all-inclusive term referring to serious music

<u>Classical</u>: musical style period, 1750-1825 approximately (Capital C used in this text to distinquish usage from all-inclusive term of classical music.)

<u>notation</u>, <u>notes</u>: symbols used in music to designate pitch

<u>octave</u>: interval formed by two notes of the same name, one note having twice the number of vibrations per second as the other, i.e. A to A^1

<u>interval</u>: distance between two notes

<u>musical staff</u>: relational grid, five equidistant parallel lines, used in music to indicate relative positions of pitches

 musical staff

<u>clef</u>: symbol used in music to designate a particular pitch reference point on a musical staff

<u>treble clef</u>: also known as the G clef, specifies the note G on the staff:

<u>bass clef</u>: also known as the F clef, specifies note F on musical staff:

ledger, leger lines: extra lines added to notes above and below the staff in order to easily read notes that move above or below the staff:

grand staff: combination of two staffs with treble and bass clefs; used in music for the piano:

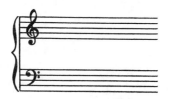

middle C: note where bass and treble clefs meet in the grand staff (see page 8)

movable C clef: movable clef used to specify the note middle C as reference point on the musical staff:

step: distance between two consecutive notes, the interval of a second (2nd)

half step: the octave is divided into twelve equal divisions called half steps; smallest standard interval in classical music

whole step: equal to two half steps

accidentals: symbols used to raise or lower a given pitch-- sharp (#), flat (b), or return an altered pitch to non-altered, natural (♮)

sharp: #, raises note in music one half step, i.e. C# is one half step higher than C

flat: b, lowers note in music one half step, i.e. Bb is one half step lower than B

natural:♮ , returns alterned note (note with an
accidental) to normal pitch, i.e. C# to C♮, or just C
(lowers C# to C)

major scale: scale using a specific pattern of whole
and half steps within the octave: ws. ws, hs, ws, ws,
ws, hs

scale: ordering a series of pitches from lowest to
highest or highest to lowest

tonic: tonal center or I position of a scale, in C major
the note C

key: scale or music oriented around a particular pitch,
i.e. key of C major

key signature: sharps or flats placed at beginning of
staff to the right side of the clef sign to indicate
key of piece (the accidentals to be played)

chromatic scale: scale using all twelve half steps in
the octave

chromaticism, chromatic: movement in half steps

Chapter II

Duration

One of the most essential ingredients of modern popular music is a good <u>beat</u> or pulse. However, beat is only one of the many parts that constitute the aspect of <u>duration</u> in music. Also important to the overall concept of duration are rhythm, speed or tempo, the fundamental movement of the music, and also the absence of sound or silence. To fully comprehend the somewhat complex <u>relational</u> system of musical duration it is necessary to directly experience the wide variety of the aspects of duration covered in this chapter. Through class experiences and an awareness of the import of the aspects of duration on everyday life you can further understand the significance of musical motion.

The <u>duration</u> of sound, in other words the length of the sound (or notes), is also organized as a relational system. Historically a regularly recurring beat or pulse, notes with the same duration, set the basis for most of the music written and performed today. If you were to clap a rhythm of a familiar song you would be able to quickly establish the basic pulse "behind" the musical motion of the tune. For instance, clap the rhythm to the song "Twinkle, Twinkle, Little Star."

It should be very easy to establish a steady pattern of "beats" using the first few words as a guide. Now if you walk around the room taking one step for each beat, but clapping the <u>rhythm</u> of the music (words) you will see the difference between pulse and rhythm. <u>Rhythm</u> could be defined as the <u>regular</u> <u>movement</u> of the music, which distinguishes it from beat as rhythm is not necessarily "notes with the same duration." Rhythm in vocal music or poetry generally follows the pattern of the words. In the example below your feet set the beat; your hands clap the rhythm. This can be illustrated with lines of different length.

rhythm: (clapping)	Twin kle	Twin kle	Lit tle	Star

| beat:
(walking) | | | | | | | | | |

As you can see the beat and rhythm of this song are the same except for the last word, "star", of the first

phrase, "are", of the second phrase, <u>et cetera</u>. Another
song with which this can be tried is "My country 'tis
of thee." Here the rhythm is more varied while the first
three words still set up the basic pulse.

My	coun	try	'tis		of	thee,	Sweet	land	of

lib		er	ty,	of	thee	I	sing.

On the words, "tis of thee" and "lib-er-ty" the
rhythm continues over two beats ("tis" and "lib") and
on the word "of" and the syllable "er" the rhythm is
shorter than the beat. The last word, "sing" lasts for
three beats. Obviously this system of using lines to
indicate rhythm is somewhat confusing and we will shortly discuss rhythmic notation.

There is also a basic difference to these two
songs, "Twinkle, Twinkle, Little Star" and "My Country
'tis of Thee", in how the beats are <u>organized</u>. The
organization of beats into equal time units in music is
called <u>meter</u>. In "Twinkle" the feeling of the beat when
it is clapped is: ONE, two, ONE two. Where the emphasis
is placed on the first beat of every two beats. This
<u>accenting</u> of a particular beat sets up a meter or metri-
cal pattern. In this particular case <u>duple</u> meter, or
meter based on a division of twos.

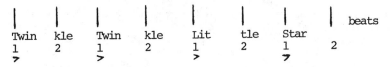

Twin	kle	Twin	kle	Lit	tle	Star		beats
1	2	1	2	1	2	1	2	
>		>		>		>		

accent marks: > [emphasis on first beat]

The unit formed by two beats in this particular
meter is called a <u>measure</u>. Measures are equal units of
time set up by specific meters.

Another form of duple meter is a piece having four
beats to a measure:

| | | | | | | | | | | | beats
Ma ry had a Lit tle lamb, Lit tle lamb,
1   2   3   4   1   2   3   4   1   2   3   4
>   (>)   >   (>)   >   (>)

Here there is a primary <u>metrical</u> <u>accent</u> on the
first beat and a secondary accent on the third beat.
This divides the measure into two groups of two beats
and thus is still considered to be a form of duple
meter. "Twinkle" could also be done in four beats.

Twin kle, Twin kle, Lit tle Star
1   2   3   4   1   2   3   4
>   (>)   >   (>)

However, if we return to the song "My Country 'tis
of Thee" you can see an example of triple meter or
division in threes. In music to divide groups of beats
into equal time units (measures) we use the <u>bar</u> <u>line</u>
(|).

My   coun try | 'tis   of thee, Sweet land of |
1   2   3 | 1   2   3 | 1   2   3 |
> | > | >

lib   er ty, | of   thee I | sing. |
1   2   3 | 1   2   3 | 1   2   3 |
> | > | >

Here accents fall on the first beat of every three.

However, we do not use lines or numbers to notate
our rhythm. Over many years a system has been derived
that enables the composer and performer to notate
rhythms very accurately. As with our system of pitch
notation the rhythmic notation system is relational,
that is, each note is related to every other note in
value (duration, length).

The basic note value of our rhythmic system is the
<u>whole note</u>: o , which we divide into other notes of
different values based on a system of <u>divisions</u> of <u>twos</u>
and <u>threes</u>. Let us examine the division of twos first:

23

A whole note may be divided
into two <u>half</u> notes: o = ♩♩

A half note may be divided
into two <u>quarter</u> notes: ♩ = ♩♩

A quarter note may be divided
into two <u>eighth</u> notes: ♩ = ♪♪ or ♫   *

An eighth note may be divided
into two <u>sixteenth</u> notes: ♪ = ♬♬ or ♫

A sixteenth note may be divided
into two <u>thirty-second</u> notes: ♬ = ♬♬ or ♫

A thirty-second note may be divided
into two <u>sixty-fourth</u> notes: ♬ = ♬

<u>et</u> <u>cetera</u>, i.e. one-hundred and twenty-eighth
notes:

    The relational aspects of this system can be seen
further in the following chart:

1 whole note: o =

2 half notes: ♩ ♩ =

4 quarter notes: ♩♩♩♩ =

8 eighth notes: ♫♫ ♫♫ =

16 sixteenth notes:

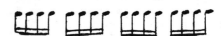

<u>et</u> <u>cetera</u>

    Very complex rhythms can be notated by using
various combinations of notes. The divisions and
combinations are infinite.

Note: Stems or "flags" may be connected by parallel
lines. The number of flags indicates the type of note.

24

For instance, a whole note could be divided into
two quarter notes and four eighth notes:

$$\circ \ = \ \text{♩♩ ♫ ♫}$$

Or a half note into one quarter and four sixteenth
notes:

$$\text{♩} \ = \ \text{♩ ♬♬}$$

Or a whole note into three eighths, two sixteenths,
and two quarter notes.

$$\circ \ = \ \text{♫ ♬♪ ♩♩}$$

et cetera

The system is expanded even more by a similar
division of threes where the note names remain the same
but the division of each "unit" or note is by three,
not two as above. Basically this means that in the space
of time occupied by one note, i.e. a whole note, three
notes are played (three half notes), instead of two.
The confusing part of the system is that we retain the
same notation and note names.

The division of threes or "triplets" is normally
indicated in the music by a small number 3 placed above
or below the triplet.

Division of threes:

A whole note may be divided $\circ \ = \ \text{♩♩♩}_3$
into three half notes:

A half note may be divided $\text{♩} \ = \ \text{♩♩♩}_3$
into three quarter notes:

A quarter note may be divided $\text{♩} \ = \ \text{♫♪}_3$
into three eighth notes:

An eighth note may be divided
into three sixteenth notes:
et cetera

25

A more comprehensive chart shows the rhythmical division of twos (duple) and threes (triple).

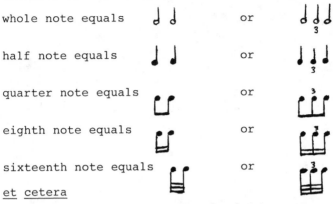

whole note equals ... or ...

half note equals ... or ...

quarter note equals ... or ...

eighth note equals ... or ...

sixteenth note equals ... or ...

et cetera

There are several other aspects of notation that need to be introduced. Since music is not all continuous sound we need an indication for silence in music. The symbols that stand for equivalent time values of silence to notes they represent are called rests. The following chart demonstrates the types of rests and their equivalent notes on the musical staff.

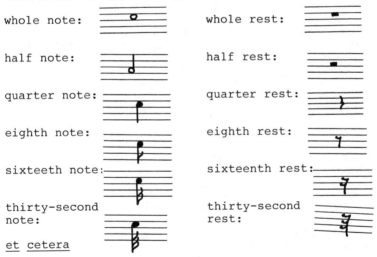

whole note: whole rest:

half note: half rest:

quarter note: quarter rest:

eighth note: eighth rest:

sixteeth note: sixteenth rest:

thirty-second note: thirty-second rest:

et cetera

Rests may be used with either duple or triple divisions of the beat.

In conjunction with either a note: ♩. or a rest 𝄼·
a <u>dot</u> may be used in rhythmic notation to lengthen the
value of the note or rest by one half the original
value. For instance, if a quarter note is equal to one
beat a <u>dotted</u> quarter note would be equal to one and
one-half beats.

♩.
1+½

And a dotted quarter rest equal to one and one-half
beats of rest.

𝄼·
1+½

Another way this can be indicated in music is
through the use of the tie (⌒). The tie is only used
with notes not with rests.

or

Ties are sometimes used to cross over bar lines
in the music.

To completely understand the notational system
used to indicate duration we must return to a discussion
of meter. IF the song "Twinkle, Twinkle, Little Star"
is written in musical notation the rhythm looks like
this.

♩ ♩ | ♩ ♩ | ♩ ♩ | 𝅗𝅥 |
1   2 | 1   2 | 1   2 | 1   2|

For the performer to understand the composer's
intentions, he must know the <u>meter</u> that the composer
wants to use because this will affect the accent patterns and expressive motion of the music. For this
purpose a <u>meter signature</u> is placed at the beginning of
the musical staff, right after the clef sign and key
signature. The meter signature indicates two specific
things: the top number tells <u>how many</u> beats are in each
measure; the bottom number tells <u>what kind</u> of note value
will represent the beat.

27

For instance:

In this case there are <u>two</u> beats in the measure (top number), and the quarter note (bottom number 4) gets the beat. (You can consider this like a fraction: 2/4 or two quarters.)

Now let us consider "Twinkle, Twinkle, Little Star" with a meter signature.

Twin kle, Twin kle, Lit tle Star

The meter signature indicates specifically that there should be two beats in each measure and that the quarter note gets the beat. As long as there is always the equivalent of two quarter notes per measure (made up of notes or rests) the music in "two-four" meter will be correct.

Let us take a brief look at another meter, using the same rhythm and tune as before, but with four beats to a measure and a change in accents.

This type of meter change using the same tune can change the basic rhythmic motion of a piece. Especially in more complicated melodies where subtler changes in meter can alter the expressive movement of a melody a great deal.

"Four-four: (4/4) time can also be noted on the staff as "common" time represented by a capital C.

Note: The third beat in four-four time has a secondary metrical accent. Here indicated by (>).

"My Country 'tis of Thee" is written in triple (three-beat) meter.

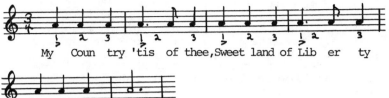

(Note the use of the dotted quarter in the second and fourth measures.)

Even with the use of a different rhythm each measure must conform to the meter signature. If you figure it out carefully there are three beats (equivalent to three quarter notes) in each measure of "My Country 'tis of Thee". The meter signature is usually only indicated at the very beginning of a piece, and, as in the second staff above, it will not be repeated unless there is to be a change of meter within the piece.

It is important that you realize there is a difference between duple and triple meter and duple and triple divisions of the beat. An example of a piece in duple meter (2/4) that uses triple division of the beat is "Hickory, Dickory, Dock".

Hic ko ry Dic ko ry Dock   The Mouse ran up the Clock

This piece can also be used to illustrate the use of compound meters. A compound meter (as opposed to "simple" meters studied so far) is where two basic meters seem to be present at the same time. For instance, "Hickory, Dickory, Dock" in compound meter would be in 6/8 meter.

Hic ko ry Dic ko ry   Dock   The Mouse ran up the clock

Here six <u>eighth</u> notes are in each measure but the main <u>beats</u> are the first and the fourth beats giving the piece a feeling of being in duple meter. If you look back at the first example of "Hickory, Dickory, Dock" in 2/4 meter with triple division of the beat you will see that the two examples are identical, and they would be sung the same way. (Simply two different ways of representing the same thing.) So that 6/8 meter really seems like two beats of three, duple AND triple meter combined. Often if this type of compound meter is used with a fast moving piece the beat will be performed as if in "two", i.e. two beats per measure, and the performer will subdivide the two beats into three each, in his head. (Note placement of accents.)

Another example of compound meter would be 9/8, which has a feeling of three groups of three.

Or 12/8, which has a feeling of four groups of three.

Another type of meter is <u>asymmetrical</u> meter, which is really a type of compound meter with unequal divisions. An example of this type of meter is 5/4. Here it is divided either in a group of two and a group of three (note the accents) or a group of three and a group of two.

or:

An aspect of rhythm that is used a great deal in Jazz and for contrast in other forms of music is <u>syncopation</u>. Syncopation occurs when the accents or

30

notes are on the weak beats of the measure or in between the beats.

Accents off the main beat.

Note the use of the tie (⌒) across the bar line and in the middle of the bar across beats.

Or:

Here the <u>notes</u> fall in between the beats.

One of the most important things to remember about the system of rhythmical notation is that the length of each note is <u>relative</u>. What sets the speed of the notes in music is called <u>tempo</u>. Depending on the tempo (speed) of a piece of music a quarter note <u>could</u> be very long or very short, and all the other notes would then relate to the <u>note that gets the beat</u>.

Frequently a composer will indicate the tempo he wants the work to be played at on the score just above the first staff.

Allegro

Here the tempo is <u>fast</u> and the quarter note gets the beat, i.e. the quarter note will be played at a fast tempo.

Most of the music written before 1900 used Italian words for the different speeds indicated in the score. Tempo markings also often indicate a general "mood" as well as speed, i.e. allegro appassionata would mean fast and passionately. In modern times the native language of the composer has prevailed over Italian in notating scores so that today you would likely see words like "fast", "slow", "heavy" as tempo indications on a score written by an American composer. However, since you will encounter the Italian frequently on programs

31

it is valuable to be familiar with the most commonly used tempo markings.

> Grave: very, very slow, solemn
> Largo: very slow, broad
> Lento: slow
> Adagio: slow, "at ease"
> Andante: slow but moving, walking
> Andantino: a little faster than andante
> Moderato: moderately
> Allegretto: somewhat slower than allegro; moderately fast
> Allegro: fast, "cheerful"
> Vivace: lively
> Presto: very fast
> Prestissimo: very, very fast (as fast as possible)

These terms are listed from the slowest to the fastest. They may also be preceded by several other terms to specify even further the composer's intentions.

> meno: less, i.e. meno allegro (less fast--a little slower
> piu: more, i.e. piu allegro (more fast--faster)
> ma non troppo: not too much, i.e. allegro ma non troppo (fast but not too fast)
> poco: a little, i.e. poco allegro (a little allegro, not so fast)
> molto: very, i.e. molto allegro (very fast)

During the composition if a composer wants the piece to change tempo he must also indicate it on the score. Some of the terms for changes in tempo are:

> accelerando: to speed up, get faster; abbreviated: acc. or accel.
> rallentando: to slow down; abbreviated: rall.
> ritardando: to slow down; abbreviated: rit. or ritard.
> a tempo: return to tempo (used after tempo has been changed)
> tempo primo: return to first tempo
> poco a poco: little by little, i.e. poco a poco accelerando (little by little get faster)

Tempo indications tend to be rather general in nature and one composer's conception of an allegro may be vastly different from another's. Usually it is left to the performer and the style of music being performed to determine exactly how fast a work will be played.

32

However in 1816 a man named Malzel invented a device called the metronome. This unique device, both a blessing and a bane to all musicians, ticks nonchalantly onward at a steady number of beats per minute despite all attempts by frustrated musicians to prove it wrong. It does give the composer a very accurate indication of speed and can be adjusted to tick from approximately forty beats per minute, a very slow tempo, to about two hundred beats per minute, a very fast tempo.

While this is a very general introduction to meter and rhythm it should give you the basis for understanding how the system works. You will be given ample opportunities in class to experiment with this aspect of music.

Melodic and Accompanying Rhythms

While we have discussed rhythm as a function separate from music you should always remember that it is always an essential element of the expressive motion of a piece of music. As a simple means of analysis rhythm could be divided into three basic forms, each derived from the music itself: melodic rhythm, accompanying rhythm, and beat.

The concept of beat and meter has been covered in some detail but it is important to remember the significance of <u>metrical</u> <u>accents</u> in a piece of music. While they may not be obvious they are inherent to the concept of movement in music.

An "accompanying rhythm" is a rhythm that is also a steady rhythmic pattern though differing from the beat. Accompanying rhythms tend to be repetitive patterns within the basic pattern of the meter and beat. A typical accompanying rhythm would be simply a steady pattern of notes faster than the beat, i.e. eighth notes (twice as fast as the quarter note beat) or sixteenth notes (four times as fast as the quarter note beat, or four to each beat).

etc.

or:

etc.

Off-beats or syncopation could also be used as an accompanying rhythm. Or any type of alternating rhythmic pattern that is steadily repetitive:

 etc.

or:

 etc.

et cetera

The melodic rhythm refers to the rhythm of the melody. This can be very free, or repetitive over a longer period of time as in stanzas of songs. If you pick any song and clap the rhythm of the words, you will be clapping the melodic rhythm. As seen in "Twinkle, Twinkle, Little Star" this can be a very simple pattern. Or as in "Oh, Sussanna" below it can be more complicated. Melodic rhythms of classical works tend to be more complex and varied than in popular songs. If you listen carefully to varying types of music you should be able to begin to discern these three main types of rhythmic motion in music: beat, accompanying rhythms, and melodic rhythms.

Chapter II: Glossary

beat: the regular pulse in most music

rhythm: regular movement of the music, distinguished from the beat in that rhythm is not necessarily "notes with the same duration" or "a steady pulse"

meter: the organization of beats into equal units of time

duple meter: meter based on a division of twos, i.e. 2/4; 4/4; et cetera

triple meter: meter based on a division of threes, i.e. 3/4; 3/8; et cetera

rhythmic notation: notes and rests, see pages 24-27

dotted note or dotted rest: $\boldsymbol{\downarrow}$. , $\boldsymbol{\gamma}$. , dot adds one half again the value of the note or rest to the note or rest

tie: ($\frown$) "ties" two notes together to produce a continuous sound

meter signature: sign placed on the first staff of a piece of music immediately after the clef sign and key signature indicating the meter of the piece, i.e. 2/4

compound meters: music where two basic meters seem to be present, i.e. 6/8, 9/8, et cetera, see pages 29-30

asymmetrical meters: basically a compound meter with unequal divisions, i.e. 5/4, 7/4; et cetera, see page 30

syncopation: when either the accents are on the weak beats of the measure, or the notes are in between the beats, "off-beats"

tempo: speed in music;

tempo markings: see page 32

melodic rhythm: rhythm of the melody

accompanying rhythm: repetitive rhythm pattern that is different from a simple, steady beat, see pages 33-34 for examples

35

Chapter III

Dynamics

The term <u>dynamics</u> refers to the loudness or softness of the sound, or more correctly, the <u>intensity</u>.
In a scientific sense this is directly related to the
amplitude of the sound wave.

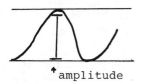

↑amplitude

The wider the amplitude of the wave the louder the
sound.

In music dynamics are a very important consideration in regard to the performance or interpretation of
a composition. Without any change in dynamics or intensity a piece becomes boring very quickly. As you will
see in the historical portion of this text the use of
dynamics varies a great deal depending on the style of
the music and when it was written.

You have already seen the importance of the
metrical accent or beat accent in relationship to the
musical beat. This is particularly important in the
popular and jazz styles of modern music. If popular
music did not use strong beats or metrical accents, it
would quickly lose the interest of many listeners.

The use of dynamics, in other words, the overall
conception in the music of loud and soft, is also very
important. In some forms of popular music the general
performance medium seems to be the louder the better.
But in classical music the subtle relationships between
louds and softs are very important to the overall
expressive effect and quality of the music.

In classical music the terms we use to indicate
dynamics and changes in intensity in the musical scores
are again taken from long historical usage. These terms
are from Italian derivation and are also relational
terms according to the particular composer's usage and
the individual performer's interpretation.

The two most common terms used in music for intensity are "forte" meaning loud, and "piano" meaning soft.
By themselves these two terms limit the range of dynamic
expression to very general terms. However, it is possible to modify each of these dynamic markings to set up
a very extensive range of suble expression from very,
very loud to very, very soft.

As a medium range the term "mezzo" meaning half,
is placed before either piano or forte. "Mezzo forte"
means half loud, and it is somewhat softer than forte.
"Mezzo piano" means half soft, and it is somewhat louder
than piano, but not as loud as mezzo forte. If we set
up a scale showing the range of expression from soft to
loud, you can get a beginning perspective of the dynamics discussed so far.

piano	mezzo piano	mezzo forte	forte
soft	half soft	half loud	loud

We can extend this range even further at each end
by using the Italian suffix indicating the superlative:
"issimo". Thus a "forte" becomes "fortissimo" and means
very loud, and a "piano" becomes "pianissimo" and means
very soft. And extended even further by adding more
"issis". Thus we can have a fortississimo or very, very
loud; or even a pianississississimo or very, very, very
soft. Composers have been known to get a bit carried
away with additions of "issis" to their music with up
to as many as five or six, i.e. fortississississississi-
mo!

Luckily these dynamics can be abbreviated by a form
of musical shorthand. The term forte can be substituted
on a score (set of musical parts or staffs) with the
letter "f" under the staff, piano with a "p", and mezzo
with an "m". And for each "issi" that the composer uses
another "f" or "p" respectively is added to the shorthand. Thus our scale of musical intensity is considerably expanded. (See table of dynamic markings in
Glossary.)

The symbols "p", "f", "mp", "fff", et cetera, are
placed under (or over) the staff on a piece of music.
These indicate to the performer at what point there
will be a general change in intensity (see score next
page).

It is also necessary to have a means of getting from one dynamic level to another. The term "crescendo" means to get louder and can be abbreviated "cresc." Decrescendo" means to get softer and is abbreviated "decresc." Another term used to indicate getting softer is "diminuendo" and it can be shortened to "dimin." or preferably "dim." These terms can also be modified by a variety of Italian words, some of which you became familiar with in the chapter on duration. "Molto cresc." would mean to get <u>very</u> loud. "poco a poco dim." would mean to get soft <u>little</u> <u>by</u> <u>little</u>, and "piu crescendo" would mean <u>more</u> crescendo. Another Italian term often used as a modifier is "sempre", meaning "always". So that "sempre crescendo" would mean always get louder.

There is also a shorthand notation in music for getting louder and softer.

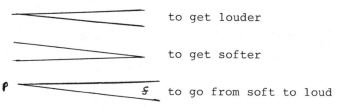

to get louder

to get softer

to go from soft to loud

An advantage of these "shorthand" symbols is the capability of using them to indicate exactly how long the crescendo or decrescendo will last. The following score example shows the use of a variety of dynamic markings.

You are already familiar with metrical accents in conjunction with beats in music, but another type of accent, the <u>dynamic accent</u>, is used as a means of adding a wider range of dynamic character to the music. These accents can take a variety of forms. Often an accent mark (>) will be placed over or under a note to indicate to the performer that he should emphasize that particular note/notes.

Dynamic accents that relate to the Italian word "forte" are the terms sforzando" or sforzato" which mean forced. These two words can be abbreviated in music under (or over) the note to be emphasized like this:

"Fortepiano" is another term that is a type of dynamic accent. It means that a note should be played first loudly and then suddenly softly. (See score on page 39 for examples of dynamic accents.)

Although many symbols and terms are used today to indicate to the performer general and specific ideas for dynamic interpretation, in the final analysis most of the subtle changes of intensity added to the music by the sensitive performer are a matter of individual interpretation according to the style of music being performed. It takes a marvelous expressive sensitivity to be able to add the shadings and colors and intensity to the music of the masters in a first rate musical performance. The greatest musicians are those who have developed this fine sensitivity to the music they play.

Chapter III: Glossary

dynamics: the loudness or softness of sound in music (intensity)

forte: Italian term for loud

piano: soft

mezzo: half

-issimo: Italian superlative--very

crescendo: to ger louder

decrescendo: to get softer

diminuendo: to get softer

poco a poco: little by little

sempre: always

dynamic accent: marking in music to emphasize a specific note

accent mark: >

sforzando; sforzato: type of dynamic accents--"forced"

fortepiano: dynamic accent; to play loudly then softly

Table of dynamic markings

pianississimo	ppp	very, very soft
pianissimo	pp	very soft
piano	p	soft
mezzo piano	mp	half soft
mezzo forte	mf	half loud
forte	f	loud
fortissimo	ff	very loud
fortississimo	fff	very, very loud
crescendo	cresc.	get louder
decrescendo	decresc.	get softer
diminuendo	dim.	get softer
accent	>	emphasize note
sforzando, sforzato	sfz, sf	emphasize note
fortepiano	fp	loud then soft

Chapter IV

Timbre

Tone quality or the timbre (pronounced tam ber) of
a particular instrument is very difficult to describe
in words, yet most people can learn to distinguish the
quality of sounds from a wide range of instruments.
Someone might describe a violin's tone as being warm,
or perhaps brilliant. But unless you have heard the
sound of a violin you will not really understand what
that person means by its tone quality, because a trumpet
can also be warm and brilliant.

There are several factors that affect the quality
of tone that a particular instrument produces. One
factor is the material from which the instrument is
constructed. A metal instrument will sound much different from a wooden instrument. The shape of the instrument and the way it is made will also affect the tone
quality. One instrument manufacturer or maker can produce a wide variety of timbres in his instruments different from the timbres of instruments built by another
maker. Perhaps even more important to the tone quality
is how the sound is produced on the instrument: a drum
is hit, a horn blown, a violin bowed or plucked, et
cetera.

Scientifically the quality of sound changes according to the amount and the relationship of the overtones
that the instrument produces. All the factors listed
above will affect the overtones, thus producing different tone colors.

When a note is produced on an instrument, it is
because a part of the instrument has been set into
vibrations that produce audible pitch. As you learned
in chapter one, the number of vibrations per second
affect the pitch. In all instruments the vibrating body,
whether it is a pipe, string, or drum head, also will
vibrate in segments producing secondary vibrations call-
overtones.

In ancient Greece, Pythagoras, the famous mathe-
matician, discovered that plucked strings would vibrate
not only along their entire length, but also in segments
that were related proportionally to the whole string.
These "secondary" vibrations in the string produce
higher pitches that affect the tone color of the sound
greatly, but we generally cannot aurally distinguish

43

the secondary vibrations from the main tone.

As an example of this basic concept, if we take the string WX we used in the first chapter you will be able to see how the string also vibrates in smaller segments.

440 vib./sec.

Fundamental tone: string vibrating along entire length.

Overtone: string vibrating in half, overtone pitch 880 vib./sec.

Overtone: string vibrating in fourths: overtone pitch 1760 vib./sec.

(To illustrate clearly all the different overtones produced in a single string and how they combine to form a distinctive tone would require complicated electronic equipment. For a brief discussion of the overtone series turn to the end of this chapter.)

Each instrument has a distinctive pattern and prominence of overtones when it is played. One trumpet will sound different from another, or one violin from another. Even those made by the same maker will have subtle differences in tone color. Our ears are quick to notice these differences even though it is impossible to differentiate all the minute segments of sound that make up a particular tone quality.

To really understand timbre it is necessary to look at all of the instruments that are used in classical music today. How each individual instrument produces sound and how the instruments are grouped together in symphonies and other ensembles are important to the quality of sound produced.

Musical instruments are grouped together into different families of instruments that produce sound in the same basic manner. The four main families of instruments are the strings, woodwinds, brass, and percussion. Often the human voice is designated as a separate "family". It also seems easier to classify the keyboard instruments into a separate group, even though they do fit conveniently into one or more of the other families. And today we recognize the important growth and use of electronic instruments as an essential part of classical music.

Voice

Probably the first instrument to be explored by man was his own voice. Considered even today to be the purest form of expression, the voice has always been an important element in the classical music world. Voices are normally classified according to their range. The primary divisions being soprano (S), alto (A), tenor (T), and bass (B) parts: SATB. However in classical music and in particular opera there are many other divisions which partially denote range, but also refer to the quality of the individual voice. Thus we have coloratura sopranos, lyric sopranos, dramatic sopranos, mezzo-sopranos, contraltos, contratenors, baritones, basso profundos, et cetera (here arranged basically from highest to lowest). We even have Wagnerian sopranos, Irish tenors, and other more specific titles to help us distinguish one singer's voice from another's.

Vocal Ensembles

Besides the popular SATB chorus a wide variety of different vocal ensembles have been used throughout Western music history. Many choruses have more parts than the standard four part form, often dividing the different voice parts into two and three separate sections. Also it has been popular to divide the choir into two or even more separate groups of four parts each. This is sometimes referred to as the double chorus or polychoric writing (many choruses).

Opera, which is basically a play set to music, uses a wide variety of vocal ensembles ranging from simple duets, trios, and quartets to more complicated sextets, octets, and full choruses.

Some choirs specialize in a type of singing that has a unique timbre: the a cappella choir. This is where the chorus sings without any instrumental accompaniment. When it is done well, it is a wonderfully pure sound to hear.

String Family

The primary stringed instruments used in the orchestra are the violin, viola, violoncello (cello), and double bass or contrabass (string bass or bass). These instruments are played by either plucking the strings or drawing a bow across the strings to set them into vibration.

violin, viola, cello, string bass

For the strings to vibrate freely when they are set in motion, they are suspended by a bridge, which also transfers the vibrations to the body of the instrument. The strings are attached at one end to pegs, which enable the player to tune the instrument, and at the other end they are anchored in a tailpiece, which in turn is attached to the body of the instrument. In order to produce different pitches on the instrument a player must use his fingers to "stop" the string by placing them on the string and pushing the string onto the fingerboard. The violin bow is made of a special flexible wood from South America and the part that touches the string is, indeed, horsehair. The hair of horses bred in very cold climates (Canada, Siberia) is used because it is coarse and grips the string better. The strings are made of metal or sheep's gut (not cat gut) wound with metal. The string instruments of the violin

46

family do not use frets like the guitar and banjo. The performer must memorize the distances on the instrument fingerboard for correct intonation. (As an item of interest: The violin and fiddle are the same instrument. Only the style of playing is different.)

There is a difference in the size of the string instruments of the violin family. The violin is the smallest, viola next largest, then the cello, and finally the string bass is the largest. It should be noted that the <u>larger</u> the instrument the <u>lower</u> the the sound. It is <u>not</u> necessarily true that bigger instruments will sound louder than smaller instruments. (Compare sizes of the violin, viola, cello, and bass in the picture on page 46.) Thus the violin is the highest pitched and the string bass the lowest pitched of the violin family.

Because of the small size of the violins and violas they can be played while standing or sitting, and are held under the left chin of the instrumentalist. Everyone plays the violin/viola "left-handed" regardless of which hand is their preferred hand. Only in extremely rare cases where there is some physical problem will that position be reversed. This is primarily due to the convenience of playing in orchestras so that violinists and violists won't run each other through with their bows.

Because of its large size the cello is played while the performer is sitting. It is supported by the player's legs (knees) and a unique device that is attached to the bottom of the cello called the end pin. The end pin enables the cellist to anchor the instrument on the floor, giving him freedom to perform. Cellists can be thankful to a certain French cellist who became too fat to hold the cello between his legs, so he developed a "pin" to help hold the instrument. It caught on, even for skinny cellists.

The double bass, also known as the string bass, contrabass, or simply bass can be played either standing, or sitting on a high stool. The "monster" of the string family is actually a mellow, very deep sounding instrument. Today it is popular in jazz groups as well as in the symphony orchestra. The bass also rests on the floor with an end pin used to anchor it.

The harp, also a member of the string family, is used occasionally in the symphony orchestra. A very

large instrument, the harp is played sitting down and
is plucked or strummed to produce sound. The harp is
the distant ancestor of the Greek lyre, which was a
much smaller hand-held instrument.

There are a number of other string instruments
that are rarely used in the orchestra, but are very
popular in other forms of music: the guitar, banjo,
and mandolin. The lute, an ancient Medieval and
Renaissance instrument has been making a comeback as
a folk instrument and for accompanying songs.

Many other instruments that fit into the string
instrument category, particularly folk instruments like
the dulcimer, are rarely used in classical music or the
symphony orchestra. These instruments are fascinating
to explore as a part of the folk heritage of the United
States and other countries.

Woodwind Family

Even though they are called woodwinds the instruments of the woodwind family are no longer all made of
wood. However, they are all instruments whose sound is
produced by the player setting a column of air in motion
by blowing into or across a pipe. The embouchure of the
player is the way he shapes his lips on the mouthpiece.

piccolo	English	Clarinet	bass	alto	bassoon
flute	Horn		clarinet	saxophone	
oboe					

48

The embouchure is very important in developing the quality of sound in a woodwind instrument. The woodwinds are played by fingering different holes or keys along the instrument's length; this produces changes in pitch. By depressing a key, or covering a fingerhole, the player changes the length of the column of air and hence changes the pitch.

The flute family consists of basically two instruments: the flute and the piccolo. Today most flutes are made of metal and use a complicated mechanism of keys to change pitches. In ancient times the flute was wooden (an example would be a fife today) and did not have keys, only holes to cover with the fingers. The piccolo, a smaller version of the flute, is higher pitched. Both of these instruments are very agile and are able to play very fast, high passages. Flutes are played by blowing across a hole in the instrument's mouthpiece. (The same effect you get in blowing across an open pop bottle.)

A group of instruments related to the flute is the recorder family. The recorder, an instrument from the Medieval and Renaissance periods, has regained popularity, especially because it is relatively easy to learn to play, and is excellent for family musical participation. Recorders are made from wood or plastic and are played in front of the performer with the player's mouth over the mouthpiece.

The <u>double reed</u> instruments are woodwinds that use a mouthpiece formed by two facing reeds that are blown through to set the air in motion.

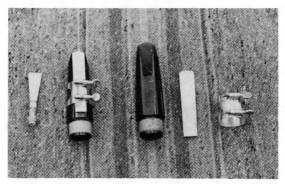

double   single reed mouthpieces and single reed
reed

The oboe is the most well known of the double reeds. It has a "nasal" tone quality. Directly related to the oboe, but lower in pitch and slightly larger, is the English Horn, which is in reality neither English nor a horn. The double reed is placed in the mouth and the player blows through it setting the opposing reeds into vibration. Both the oboe and English Horn are held in front of the player.

On the lower side of the double reed wind family are the bassoons. The bassoon is sometimes referred to as the clown of the orchestra because of its deep, resonant sound. The counterpart of the bassoon is the larger contrabassoon which plays even lower than the bassoon and is a large difficult instrument to play. The bassoon is held on an angle across the player's body and to his right side.

The _single_ _reed_ family is the most familiar of the woodwind families to the non-musician. A single reed instrument uses a mouthpiece, now usually made of plastic or hard rubber, and a single reed that vibrates against the open side of the mouthpiece. (See page 49 for a picture of the single reed and mouthpiece.)

The clarinet family consists of a wide variety of sizes of instruments. The most common clarinet is the B-flat clarinet, which is used in bands, orchestras, and many other ensembles. The clarinet is very versatile, and can play extremely rapid passages over a wide range. Other clarinets look the same as the B-flat but are slightly different in size and are pitched to different notes, i.e. the A clarinet. The bass clarinet is shaped differently from the other clarinets. It has a lovely deep tone while still retaining most of the versatility of the other clarinets.

The saxophones are also single reed instruments, and though they are rarely used in the symphony orchestra they are a very popular instrument in bands, jazz, and rock groups. Saxes come in a variety of shapes and sizes. They are generally made of metal. The most popular saxophones are the soprano, alto, tenor, and baritone.

Brass Family

Brass players produce sound by blowing air into the instrument through a mouthpiece that is either conical or cup shaped. When the player blows through

50

the mouthpiece his lips vibrate against the mouthpiece
to set the air in motion.

cup   conical
mouthpiece   mouthpiece

The brass instruments use a different method from
the woodwinds for changing pitch. Instead of holes and
keys the brass have a a series of valves, which, when
depressed, change the length of the tubing. In the case
of the trombone, the player directly changes the pitch
of the instrument by moving the slide in and out.

cornet   French Horn   baritone   tuba
trumpet
slide trombone

The most popular brass instrument is the trumpet,
which uses three <u>piston</u> valves (see above photograph)
to change the pitch. The trumpets come in a wide variety of sizes and pitches. The B-flat trumpet is the most
common, although today the C trumpet is also being used
more and more. Trumpets have a brilliant, and character-
istically "brassy" timbre. They are very popular in

bands and jazz ensembles.

An instrument that looks similar to the trumpet but is slightly shorter in length is the cornet. The cornet, softer and mellower than the trumpet, is used in England more than in the United States. Both the trumpet and cornet use cup-shaped mouthpieces.

The French Horn is a very mellow brass instrument that is related to the old hunting horn. It is shaped differently from the trumpet (see photograph below), and most French Horns use what is known as the rotary valve. The rotary valve rotates in a circular motion to change the length of the tubing rather than the up and down piston effect of the trumpet (see photograph on page 51).

The French Horn is played sitting down, with the bell of the horn resting on the performer's leg. The French Horn is the only brass instrument that uses the conical mouthpiece.

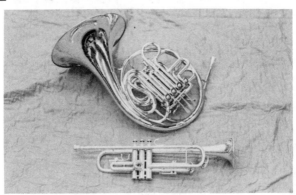

French Horn--rotary valves

Trumpet--piston valves

The trombone is a unique member of the brass family because of the use of the slide. It has a deep tone that can be very brassy or very mellow in color. The trombone uses a cup shaped mouthpiece.

The lowest of the brass instruments is the tuba. The tuba has a deep, deep sound that is often character- ized by the ohm-pah, omh-pah-pah sound of band music. The tuba uses a cup shaped mouthpiece and usually has rotary type valves. The most common tubas are the

52

E-flat bass tuba and the double B-flat contrabass tuba.

Several other brass instruments that are commonly used in bands and other ensembles are the flugelhorn, similar to the cornet but larger in size; the baritone horn, shaped like the tuba but smaller and pitched approximately in the trombone range; and the sousaphone, basically a tuba for marching.

Percussion Family

The percussion family consists of a wide variety of instruments in which the sound is produced by striking or shaking the instrument. They are probably the oldest form of instrument used except for the human voice. Long before any other instruments were developed man had probably begun to beat rhythms with sticks on hollow logs.

Percussion instruments can be divided into several categories. The most common division is into those instruments that have definite pitch and those that do not. However, we can also divide the percussion family into other smaller sections: metal instruments, wooden instruments, drums, keyboard or mallet percussion, et cetera.

The immense variety of percussion instruments precludes any attempt to cover them effectively in part of a chapter. The main types of percussion will be covered to give you a perspective of the kinds used in orchestras and bands today. Almost anything that can be struck or shaken is considered a potential instrument by composers today.

The most familiar percussion instruments are the drums. The kettledrums or timpani (tympani) are "pitched" percussion instruments that can be tuned with a pedal mechanism attached to the bottom of the drum. The timpani are the large "kettles", with a calfskin or synthetic drum head stretched across the instrument to create tension. The timpani are used in combinations of usually up to four drums per performer. Each timpani will be of a different size providing the potential for a wide range of pitches. For a long period of music history the timpani were the only percussion instruments used regularly in the symphony orchestra. (see picture next page)

The snare drum is the most commonly used unpitched

percussion instrument, with its "snare" sound being produced by wires that are made to come into contact with the bottom head of the instrument.

Other indefinitely pitched drums are the congo drums, bass drum, tenor drum, and bongo drums to name a few.

timpani   snare drum   bass drum

Mallet percussion are pitched percussion. The most familiar is probably the xylophone, which has tuned wooden bars that produce a hollow, "wooden" sound. The glockenspiel consists of two sets of metal bars tuned from highest to lowest. Its sound is very clear and bell-like. Other members of the mallet percussion family are the marimba, vibraphone, and the orchestral chimes. All of these instruments produce tone by being struck with mallets made of an assortment of materials from

mallet percussion

wood or plastic (hard) to yarn or soft cotton (soft). The bars on the instruments, whether metal or wooden, are ranked from highest to lowest (right to left if playing the instrument) and are tuned to the chromatic (half step scale), similar to a piano keyboard.

Some of the many other types of percussion instruments are probably already familiar to you, such as the triangle, castanets, tambourine, cymbals, sleigh bells, et cetera; but others are more likely quite strange in appearance and name: guiro, claves, gong, maracas, timbales, et cetera. To fully appreciate the myriad of percussion instruments used today in bands, percussion ensembles, and orchestras you must attend concerts of varying types of music. You might be surprised by what you see and hear.

Keyboard Instruments

The full name of the piano is the "pianoforte", meaning soft-loud (from the Italian, because it was the first keyboard instrument, besides the organ, that was capable of a wide range of dynamics). It is a very versatile instrument used in many different ensembles, is the major accompanying instrument, and is also perhaps the one universal solo instrument. The piano is really a combination of two instruments. It is a string instrument because the sound is produced by setting strings into vibration, and it is a percussion instrument because the strings are struck by a felt hammer. The complicated mechanical connections that enable a pianist to play the instrument from a single keyboard

Grand piano--piano-forte

55

produce, with a sensitive touch, a most exquisite sound. The piano has an extensive range covering more than seven octaves. Of all the instruments played today, the piano is probably the most technically demanding on the performer. The quality and level of difficulty of the literature written for piano has become highly developed over the last two centuries.

The organ, a favorite instrument for many centuries, is most often associated with church music, although today it is used in other ensembles as well. The pipe organ is the ultimate instrument of this type and the finer instruments are very large, with great ranks of pipes and three or more keyboards, requiring great dexterity and knowledge to perform. Today, of course, we have electric organs in many styles and types, but the purists still prefer to listen to the better sounding pipe organs in the massive old cathedrals. The organ is a wind instrument in which air is released into pipes through a series of mechanisms that are eventually attached to the keyboard. A complex array of sounds can be produced by varying the number and type of pipes that sound at any given moment. The organ is one of the few instruments in which feet play an important role, since there is a complete separate keyboard for the organist to play on with his feet.

harpsichord

The harpsichord was very popular during the late Renaissance and Baroque periods (1500-1750). It is a keyboard instrument in which strings are set into motion

by being plucked by tiny quills when the keys are depressed. It has no sustaining power and no real dynamic
range, and after the piano was introduced, it became
much less popular. Today it is used primarily to perform
pieces from the period of music history when it was THE
keyboard instrument.

Electronic Instruments

Since the late nineteeth century the use of new
and unusual instruments has spread by leaps and bounds.
With this growth came the eventual use of electronics
in the musical world. The use of radio, records, tape
recordings, and finally television and the movies has
brought about considerable change in the performance
and production of music. Soon these electronic media
were used in actual musical works: tape recorders added
new sounds to the symphony orchestra--anything that
could be taped could be used again on the concert stage,
from mechanical sounds to natural sounds like thunder
and birds singing. The music or electronic synthesizer
has added more dimensions to the production of music
with the use of microtones (tones smaller than a half
step), syne tones (pure sound, no overtones), and complex rhythms and harmonies perfectly blended with the
precision of electronics. The computer had also found
its way into the music world. When coupled with the
synthesizer many new sound combinations are capable of
being produced through the use of a wide diversity of
data to program the computer. It is also used today by
modern composers to plan and even help "compose" a piece
of music. With modern technology the world of music has
has taken many new directions. We can only speculate
what "new" instruments and effects will be possible
tommorrow.

Instrumental Ensembles

In America the most popular instrumental ensemble
for junior high and senior high school students is the
band. Both the marching and concert bands are extremely
popular as well as pep bands, jazz bands, rock groups,
drum and bugle corps, and other wind, brass, and percussion ensembles. However, in classical music the most
important large ensemble is the orchestra. For this
reason this text will focus on the symphony orchestra
and other string, wind, brass, and percussion ensembles
common to the classical idiom. (In recent years the
concert bands and wind ensembles have turned more and
more toward performing modern classical music and

transcriptions of the "old masters").

The orchestra can vary greatly in size depending on the piece of music performed, and often the instrumentation (instruments used in the ensemble) will vary greatly; but there is a basic grouping that is fundamental to the orchestra sound. A FULL size symphony orchestra (e.g. Chicago Symphony) will have approximately one hundred performers distributed in the following sections: 18 first violins, 16-18 second violins, 10 violas, 10 cellos, 8 string basses, 3 flutes and piccolo, 3 clarinets and bass clarinet, 2 or 3 oboes and English Horn, 2 or 3 bassoons and contrabassoon, 3 trumpets, 4 French Horns, 3 trombones, 1 tuba, 4 percussionists, 2 harps, and piano. Of course each orchestra varies greatly depending on the pieces being performed and the instruments available at the time. Often smaller school and community orchestras have to make do with much smaller and less diverse ensembles.

The arrangement of the instrumentalists on stage is an important consideration, usually made by the conductor. Below is a diagram of one popular seating arrangement for orchestra. Another common seating is with the cellos and second violins changing positions indicated on the diagram.

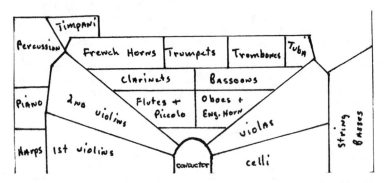

While the orchestra is the popular large ensemble of classical music there are numerous smaller ensembles that are important to be able to recognize as well. Chamber music was named for small groups that played in the "chambre" or room. During the eighteenth and nineteenth centuries chamber music developed into one of the most important idioms of classical music.

58

The most popular chamber music ensemble is the string quartet. It comprises four string instruments: first violin, second violin, viola, and cello. (The difference between a first violin and a second violin in any ensemble is only the part that the instrumentalist plays--the instrument is the same.)

With the advent of the piano in the early eighteenth century the realm of chamber music developed considerably with this versatile instrument. The sonata for piano and another solo instrument became a very important form. A violin sonata thus is often for violin AND piano, as a clarinet sonata would be for clarinet with piano, et cetera. This has also influenced the naming of other chamber music ensembles with piano: a piano quartet is not four pianos, but one piano and violin, viola, and cello; a piano trio is for one piano, violin, and cello; et cetera.

Other popular ensembles are the brass quintet: two trumpets, French Horn, trombone, and tuba; the woodwind quintet: flute, oboe, clarinet, French Horn, and bassoon; the string orchestra: violins, violas, cellos, and basses; and numerous other instrumental combinations. Normally all ensembles are designated, except for the sonatas with piano, with the term associated with the number of instruments in the group: duos, duets, trios, quartets, quintets, sextets, septets, octets, et cetera.

As you study the various periods of music history and listen to a wide range of classical music you will become more familiar with some of these ensembles, particularly the symphony orchestra. When you attend recitals and listen to recordings you will experience some of the different timbres these instruments and ensembles can produce.

Overtone Series

The scientific basis for the overtone series is the proportional relationships set up in the secondary vibrations over a fundamental tone. In the illustration below the fundamental tone is low "C" or C_2.

Each note above this fundamental is proportionally higher by smaller and smaller intervals. The first note above the the fundamental is an octave, hence our fundamental interval, here C_2 to C_1: proportionally 1:2, i.e. if C_2 is 100 vib./sec., C_1 is 200 vib./sec. (100:200; 1:2). The next interval is smaller, a fifth, C_1 to G_1, the next strongest relationship in music, I to V (see next chapter). Here the proportional relationship is 2:3, i.e. if C_1 is 200 vib./sec., G_1 will be 300 vib./sec. (200:300, or 2:3.) Each progressive interval continues to get slightly closer together, producing at the furthest end of the series (which theoretically can continue forever) intervals smaller than a half step. The tones of the harmonic series would seem <u>out</u> <u>of</u> <u>tune</u> to your ears if played as a scale because <u>just</u> or <u>true</u> intonation, derived from the overtone series, is different from the twelve equal half steps of our current musical system. The proportional relationships do not create a system of equal half steps in the octave and certain notes of the overtone series are out of tune with <u>equal</u> <u>temperament</u>. Equal temperament, developed during the Baroque period (1600-1750), is the use of twelve equal half steps within the octave and enabled composers to use notes and keys related to the notes higher in the overtone series that would be out of tune in relation to the fundamental tone of the series and <u>just</u> intonation.

Chapter IV: Glossary

Instrument families:

Voice: Soprano, Alto, Tenor, Bass (SATB)

String: violin, viola, violoncello (cello), double bass (bass, contrabass, string bass), harp, quitar

Woodwind: piccolo, flute, clarinet, bass clarinet, oboe, English Horn, bassoon, contrabassoon, saxophones, recorders

Brass: trumpet, cornet, French Horn, trombone, baritone horn, tuba, sousaphone

Percussion:

definite pitch: percussion instruments with definite pitch, or which can be tuned, i.e. timpani, mallet percussion

indefinite pitch: having no definite pitch, i.e. most drums, cymbals, triangle, et cetera

mallet percussion: percussion played with mallets, i.e. xylophone, glockenspiel, marimba, vibraphone

Keyboard: piano, organ, harpsichord

Electronic instruments: tape recorders, synthesizer, computer

Instrumental ensembles: symphony orchestra, chamber ensembles: string quartet, sonatas with piano, piano quartet, piano trio, brass quintet, woodwind quintet (see page 59)

Terms:

a cappella: singing without accompaniment ("as in the chapel")

embouchure: position or shape of the player's mouth on mouthpiece

single reed: woodwind instruments that use a single reed that vibrates against the mouthpiece: clarinets, saxophones double reed: woodwind instruments that use a mouthpiece made of two facing reeds: oboe, English Horn, bassoon, contrabassoon

piston valves: piston action valves used to adjust the tubing length in brass instruments: trumpet, cornet, baritone

rotary valves: valve rotates to adjust tubing length in brass instruments: French Horn, tuba

slide trombone: slide used to change pitch directly

conical mouthpiece: cone shaped mouthpiece: French Horn

cup mouthpiece: cup shaped mouthpiece: all brass except French Horn

Overtones: secondary vibrations over a fundamental tone, the number and prominence of overtones affects the timbre of the instrument

timbre: tone quality to tone color

Overtone series: see page 60

Chapter V

Melody and Harmony

Melody combines both pitch and rhythm. It is the
linear or horizontal aspect of music as opposed to the
vertical element of harmony. Most of us are immediately
aware of the melody or "tune" of a popular piece of
music but in some styles of classical music the melody
can be very difficult to recognize and is often not a
tune that we could go home whistling after listening to
the piece.

We can divide melody into two basic forms: those
that are "singable" and those that are instrumentally
based. The singable melody tends to be relatively
short, has a narrow range to fit the voice, and moves
mostly by stepwise motion (up and down without skipping
notes). A good example of a singable melody is "Mary
had a Little Lamb."

An instrumental melody on the other hand tends to
have a much wider range, moves more often by leaps,
and can be relatively long-winded. An example of an
instrumental melody is from Beethoven's Violin Sonata
#5 in F major, "Spring", the first movement, Allegro:

Of course many instrumental melodies are quite
"singable" and there are certainly many songs that have
instrumental characteristics.

Melody in music is often more complicated than the
simple tunes we hum every day. A piece may have two,
three, or even more melodies and they can be varied,
combined, or disjointed throughout the piece to make
it more interesting through repetition and contrast. A

63

melody used as a main idea in a piece is called a <u>theme</u>, and can be broken down into separate ideas or <u>phrases</u>. In the Christmas Carol "Jingle Bells" the melody can be broken into as many as four separate phrases with the first and third phrases being exactly the same and the second and fourth phrases being similar.

A short theme or part of a theme may also be called a <u>motive</u> or <u>motif</u>. In "Jingle Bells" the first phrase could be called a motive (see above).

One of the most famous motives in all music is the opening four notes of Beethoven's Fifth Symphony.

Beethoven eventually develops this idea into a thirty-five minute symphony of grandiose effect.

In classical music the WAY a melody is USED is at least as important as the melody itself. Only the greatest composers were capable of developing their melodies to their utmost beauty and expressiveness.

As we study various periods of music history and you listen to many different styles of music you will, no doubt, feel that the melodies you are listening to are often different from what you usually like to hear. It is important to keep in mind the many styles of music available even today and also the differences in life style and music that hundreds of years can make on a listener's appreciation. What you think of as being terribly boring may have been the tunes a peasant whistled as he went to work in the fields during the dark ages. Taken in perspective, melodies and music of ages past can become very expressive in meaning.

Harmony

The vertical element of music is called harmony. This is basically the relationship between notes that sound _together_. However, harmony is a very complicated relationship of different groups of sounds (chords). A _chord_ is a group of three or more notes that sound together.

chords

The most common type of chord in the system of Western major/minor tonality is called the triad. The _triad_ is a three note chord built on the interval of a third. Below the triad C E G is made up of the notes C, e, one third above C, and G, one third above E.

C E G triad

Triads may be built on any note of the scale so that a scale in C major (tonic C) would have the following triads (chords) associated with it. The Roman numerals designate the different degrees or positions of the notes and chords in the scales.

The scale of D major would have these triads:

Note that each chord or triad also has the sharps that are respectively in the key of D major where they occur in the chord. You may notice if you look carefully that some of the triads are common to both the key of C major and D major, i.e. the III chord in C major is the same as the II chord in D major and

the V chord in C is the same as the IV chord in D.
These chords, called common chords, are an important
consideration in how one key eventually relates to
another in the use of modulations (changing from one
key to another in the music).

The importance of major/minor tonality is HOW the
chords within a key relate to each other. This relationship is based on the principle of consonance and
dissonance. For purposes of this text consonance in
music is a release of tension, and dissonance is tension
or the building of tension in music.

DISSONANCE DOES NOT MEAN THAT IT SOUNDS BAD!!!

Each chord in a scale of music is related to every
other chord of that scale (and other scales) through its
sound. How these chords are used will create varying
amounts of tension and release in music. You have learned that the tonic is the tonal center of a major or
minor scale. It is the point of most consonance, the
most release! The chord that is most strongly related
to the tonic, and thus creates the most dissonance
(tension) when we go to it from the tonic is the fifth
chord of a scale, called the Dominant. The relationship
of the dominant (V chord) to the tonic (I chord) has
been the most important aspect of harmony since the
18th century. The movement from the I chord to the V
chord sets tension in music and the movement back to
the one chord releases that tension. (You can hear this
obvious relationship if it is played for you on the
piano.) This principle is the basis behind the feeling
in a piece of music in major/minor tonality that it is
"going somewhere", and why you often feel uneasy if you
don't hear the end of a song. The relationship of I to
V and V to I is one of the fundamental designs of the
Classical period forms that we will look at in the next
chapter.

The main reason that the V chord is so strongly
related to the I chord in the sense of tension and
release is because of the presence in the V chord of
the "leading tone" or seventh scale degree (i.e. in C
major a B), which is half a step away from the tonic
(i.e. B going to C). If someone plays a major scale
on the piano and stops on the seventh note of the scale
most people will automatically feel a sense of frustra-
tion or incompleteness. The scale has not been "resolved", i.e. the tension set up by the final note of
the scale needs to be released by returning to the

tonic or first degree of the scale. Try playing a C
major scale on the piano (white keys from C to C, see
page 12 for a diagram of piano keyboard to help you
find C) and observe how you feel if you stop on the
note "B", seventh note. Then "resolve" it by playing
the final C. Many people will even hum the note C in an
attempt to resolve the scale themselves. This is the
principle behind the relationship of the tonic (I) and
the dominant (V) chords of music. It is also an
illustration of the fundamental principle of tension
and release in major/minor tonality.

The relationship of these two chords is only one
of a myriad of possible relationships between the chords
of a scale and also the chords of different scales.
These relationships and the way they set up a feeling
of tension and a release of that tension in major/minor
tonality is what we call the study of harmony. It can
become very, very complicated, and it takes many years
of study before a person begins to gain a perspective
of the whole sphere of harmony. If you can imagine
trying to relate all the chords of one key and then in
addition add the relationships of chords from all the
other keys, both major and three forms of minor, you
will begin to see how complicated this process can be,
all subtly related by tension and release. The important
thing to remember in listening to music is that the
composer is taking you through a web of complex relationships that to a large extent subconsciously draw
you into this concept of tension and release or dissonance and consonance.

Of course not all music is written using the
major/minor system, and, in fact, before 1600 the system was in a very, very long stage of development.
Since 1900 composers have partly moved away from the
use of major/minor tonality and used many new and
strange harmonies that have very little to do with the
specific tension and release principles of major/minor
tonality. You will see the progress of this development
in a very broad sense during the history portion of
this course.

The next time you listen to a piece of folk,
country, or rock music try to see how the harmony is
affecting you. It tends to draw you in without your
having to think about it.

Several other aspects of harmony are important to
an understanding of this vertical element of music. The

movement from one chord to another is called a chord
progression, and when a chord resolves, it is releasing
the tension it has set up by moving to a more consonant
chord. When the music changes from one key to another
it is referred to as a modulation. And a place of rest
in music, or a point of consonance is called a cadence.
The strongest cadence is the chord progression V to I
discussed above.

Chords and harmony are often used to accompany a
melody. The chords can simply follow directly below the
melody,

C. Saint Saens

or be "broken" to add interest, contrast, and movement.

Broken chords are called arpeggios.

In the progression of music history from the Middle
Ages through to modern classical music you will study a
very brief overview of the development of melody and
harmony. While this will give you a very general notion
of how the music you listen to works, it will also show
you why some types of music are more pleasing to your
ears than other types. If you had been born one thousand years ago the major/minor tonal system would have
sounded very, very strange.

Chapter V: Glossary

melody: a series of pitches combined with rhythm, the linear or horizontal aspect of music

theme: main idea in a piece of music, "the tune"

motive or motif: a short theme or part of a theme

harmony: vertical element of music, notes that sound together

chord: group of three or more notes that sound together

triad: a three note chord built on the interval of a third, i.e. C E G

tonic chord: chord built on the tonic (I) degree of the scale, i.e. in C major a chord built on C: C E G (I chord)

consonance: release of tension in music

dissonance: tension in music

dominant chord: V chord of music, chord built on the fifth note of the scale, in C major on the note G, i.e. G B D (V chord)

leading tone: seventh scale degree, "leans" (releases) toward tonic (I) scale degree

resolution: when a chord moves to another chord in the sense of tension to release

modulation: changing keys, moving from one key to another

cadence: chord progression leading to a point of rest

arpeggios: broken chords, accompanying figures (see page 68

Chapter VI

Form, Texture, and Style

Almost all music we listen to from hard rock to
the most serious classical works is organized on many
different levels. This organization is referred to as
musical form. The form of a piece of music can be very
general (as symphonic form--a piece for orchestra) or
extremely specific (as in the relationship of one theme
to another or even one note to another). In this course
we will be primarily concerned with some of the more
general, larger forms rather than the intricacies of
the smaller relationships in music, but it is important
to realize how closely all aspects of a musical composition are controlled by the composer through the musical
form.

Form in music is determined by two simple principles: repetition and contrast. Repetition helps us
remember main ideas in a piece (themes, rhythms, harmonies, et cetera); and contrast helps keep the piece
interesting by adding new ideas and material. A very
simple example of this principle can be seen in this
version of "Twinkle, Twinkle, Little Star."

Here the first four measures are repeated exactly
in the next four measures and are also exactly the same
as the last four measures. The music in measures nine
through twelve is a contrasting idea or contrasting
music. Thus "Twinkle" analyzed this way could be said
to have an AABA form. (Letters are used in music to
designate repetition and contrast of material in a
composition as a form of shorthand. Always remember
that the main idea is one of familiarity [repetition]
and new material [contrast].) AABA form could also
be notated using the repeat sign: ‖:A:‖ BA. (The repeat
sign ‖:   :‖ means to repeat the section enclosed by the
double bars and dots.) In either case, AABA or ‖:A:‖BA,
the A section is the same four measure phrase and the

phrase in measures nine through twelve is the B section, contrasting material. This analysis can be even more specific.

By looking even closer at the melodic structure you can see how even a very simple piece like "Twinkle" can have a fairly complex underlying form. We could call the first two measures the A section, as well as measures five and six, and thirteen and fourteen; measures three and four, seven and eight, and fifteen and sixteen the B section; and measures nine and ten, and eleven and twelve another contrasting section, or C. Note further the similarity between the B section (measures three and four) to the C section (measures nine and ten). Often this similarity in melodic line would be noted in form as a <u>variation</u> of a particular phrase or section, so that the C section could really be designated B^1. This results in a further reduced form of A B A B B^1 B^1 A B or ‖:AB:‖: B^1:‖ AB. Obviously even in this simple work a very complex organization can be discerned.

How much of this was planned by the composer is impossible to know, but the principle remains the same, one of repetition (similar music) and contrast (different music), whatever the level of formal analysis.

The type of musical composition being played can be considered the broadest sense of musical form. A symphonic form is simply a large work for orchestra composed of several sections called <u>movements</u>. A movement is a distinct section of a larger work that usually is combined with other contrasting movements to create the entire piece. A typical symphony would have four movements arranged: first movement, fast, A; second movement, slow, B; third movement, fast, A; fourth movement, fast, A; or ABAA form. On a program for a concert you might see a symphony by Beethoven listed as follows:

Symphony #5 in c minor

I. Allegro con brio
II. Andante con moto
III. Scherzo: Allegro
IV. Allegro

Here the primary form is the symphony and it is divided into four major sections: fast, slow, fast, fast. Usually there will be a pause between movements in a large work.

There are many different large forms like symphonic form(sonata form, tone poem, concerto, et cetera). We will discuss a variety of these as we explore the music history portion of this course. Some of these forms are composed of separate movements as in symphonic form and others are single "movements" of continuous music.

Another example of form in a very broad sense is the structure of most vocal pieces. Many popular tunes we listen to every day are musically strophic in form. Strophic form is where each stanza of a piece uses the same music but different words. The music to "America the Beautiful" is a good example of this type of form. After singing one verse we repeat the music while singing the next verse, et cetera. Vocal music where the melody and music changes with each verse is called "through-composed." Ballads are often through-composed.

Shorter works or pieces of only one movement usually have a distinct form within the movement. Binary, ternary, and alternating forms are three of the most common.

Binary form is a composition that is divided into two distinct sections: AB. Often each of these sections will be repeated resulting in an AABB or ‖:A ‖:B‖ form. It should be noted that there are rarely any breaks between sections in this type of one movement form as in larger forms like the symphony and sonata.

Ternary form is composed of three sections: ABA is an example of ternary form. Sometimes in ternary form the first section is repeated resulting in an AABA form or ‖:A‖ BA.

The alternating forms include a wide variety of possible combinations. Some examples would be ABACABA or ABACADA. Here one main idea (repetition), A, keeps returning while being alternated with contrasting sections, B, C, D, et cetera.

It is important to remember that within each large form there are smaller forms that further specify how the music is organized. To study any of these forms in great detail would take considerable time and space; however, to show how a form can be divided into smaller and smaller sections for analysis we will examine one of the most popular forms used from approximately 1750

73

to the present in classical instrumental music.

The sonata, a piece for solo instrument or solo instrument and piano, became a fairly distinct form during the Classical period (1750-1825). This work is composed usually of four separate movements: fast, slow, moderately fast, and fast. Thus the large form of the piece could be considered A B A^1 A. Within this form each movement has a specific form as well.

The first movement form, or what became known as sonata-allegro form, has three distinct sections: the Exposition, Development, and Recapitulation, basically a large A B A form. Each of these sections is further divided into various sub-structures. We will take a close look at this structure.

The exposition of sonata-allegro form is where the main ideas of the movement are stated, usually, but not always, following this form:

exposition:

1st theme	in tonic key (I)
bridge passage	modulates to dominant (V) or closely related key
2nd theme	in dominant or closely related key
codetta	short closing section

This section can have a certain flexibility to it as far as key structure and number of themes but the important factors are the move away from the tonic (I) usually to the dominant (V) thus setting up tension; and as a statement of the main ideas of the piece.

The development section is where the original ideas stated in the exposition are expanded--repetition. This section is fairly free, with the main purpose to increase the tension of the music by modulating freely away from the tonic key with an eventual return to the tonic (release of tension) at the end of the development. In this section the composer develops the themes and ideas of the exposition by varying them, adding new harmonies, using new rhythms, breaking the themes into smaller fragments, or even combining the themes, sometimes even adding new material (repetition

74

and contrast).

The recapitulation marks the return to the tonic
and a release of the tension built up in the development, and as a restatement of the original ideas
usually as they were heard in the exposition but with
some possible variation, except that there is no
modulation and the second theme remains in the tonic
key.

recapitulation:

1st theme	in tonic key
bridge passage	remains in tonic
2nd theme	tonic key
coda	closing section

Even with this detailed outline of sonata-allegro
form there are many other elements that are important
relationally in this type of movement. Often themes,
motives, accompanying passages, bridge passages, rhythms, et cetera, will all be related in a variety of
ways making the form even more complex than can easily
be diagrammed. However our ears, often unconsciously,
do relate these elements and we experience the complete
work through listening. It should be noted that although
the outline of sonata-allegro form above is fairly
specific many variations to the basic form were used by
composers, the essential parts being repetition and
contrast, and tension and release, molded into a work
of expressive beauty.

The second movement of the sonata, which is usually the slow movement, is often in sonata-allegro form
similar to the first movement form, however the development section is either very short or even non-existent
in slow movements. The slow movement may also be in the
form of theme and variations.

Theme and variations form is exactly what it sounds
like. A theme is stated and then it is varied. Usually
this is a fairly strict form with the number of measures
of the theme, and the variations being closely related.
For instance, a theme may be four measures in length
and each variation will be either four measures or some
multiple of four measures (8, 16, et cetera). A theme
and variations form could be diagrammed: A, A', A'',

A''', _et cetera_. A variation of a theme can take many
forms: the instrument that plays the theme could change,
thus there would be a change in timbre; the melody
could be changed by adding or subtracting notes or sections; the harmony changed under the melody; the rhythms
changed; _et cetera_. The composer's imagination and
musical sense would dictate what could be used in this
type of form.

Third movement form in the Classical sonata is
usually a _minuet_ _and_ _trio_ form. This is also a very
strict form that can be divided into smaller component
structures. The minuet, A, is followed by a trio, B,
and then the minuet is played _da capo_, which means the
performer goes back and repeats the minuet. The large
form then is A B A.

However, within this larger form the sections are
usually divided into two sections: a and b, both of
which are repeated. So that the first section would be
A--aabb. The trio, B, also has two repeated sections--
ccdd; but the return to the minuet is _not_ repeated:
A--ab. The whole form diagrammed would look like this:

    minuet: trio: minuet: (da capo)

    A--aabb   B--ccdd   A--ab

(Sometimes the second section of the minuet, b, has a
return to the "a" section, so that A would look like
this: A--aababa.)

The fourth movement form of the sonata was sometimes in sonata-allegro form, but could also be in
rondo form, an alternating form. Later during the
Classical period these two forms were combined into
what became known as sonata-rondo form.

Rondo form is a much less specific form and can
basically be stated as a form where a main idea or
theme recurs at various intervals throughout the movement (repetition). So that the form A B A C A would
indicate that the main idea A recurs after interruptions
by new material B and C (contrast).

The four types of movements of sonata-allegro form
will be listened to in class to give you a perspective
of the musical organizational principles of repetition
and contrast and also tension and release. When we study
the Classical period of music history you will gain an

understanding of how these forms and ideals fit into the progression of music history.

Texture

Another aspect of music that is closely related to form is the musical <u>texture</u>. Musical texture refers to the relationship of the linear (melodic) element of music to the horizontal (harmonic) element of music. There are three primary types of texture: monophonic, polyphonic, and homophonic. We will see how closely allied texture is to the historical progression of music later in the course.

<u>Monophonic</u> literally means "one sound" and refers to a piece of music with only one line of music, or one melody. If we all sang the "Star Spangled Banner" together in unison or in octaves we would be singing monophonically. There is only one melody and no harmony; singing in octaves is not considered harmony.

<u>Polyphonic</u> means "many sounds" and refers to more than one melody going on at the same time. It is important to remember that polyphony is linear or melodically oriented. The simplest example of polyphonic music is the round. If we all sang, "Row, Row, Row Your Boat", but divide into three groups and start at different times we would be singing polyphonically: there would be basically three melodies going on at the same time. (Here, of course, they would be the same melody, but at different times--still "many sounds" or polyphony.) Here is a short example of a piece of music using several different melodies.

Short example of polyphonic music
(two different melodies)

Homophonic music is melody with harmony. This is where the vertical element of music becomes more important. Most of the music you listen to is homophonic. The folk songs, rock songs, country tunes, et cetera all have a melody with accompaniment. Homophonic means literally "same sounds" and refers to the harmony following directly below the melody in a chordal fashion although homophonic music is often much more complex than that.

Musical Style

There are many elements that affect the style of a piece of music. Probably the most significant effect on style is the period of time in which a piece was written. As many of you realize, popular music styles change very rapidly. What people listen to in one decade can be completely different from what is popular in the next. Though these changes seem to be gradual at the time, it is easy to see them as we look back a few decades at the music to which our parents and grandparents listened.

In classical music we divide music history into long stylistic periods. These periods are times of change and growth, but they also have basic elements that can distinguish them from other periods. The dates are only approximate and the various styles overlap considerably. We will study each of these periods during the music history section of the course.

Greek music	600-300BC
Medieval period	400AD-1450
Renaissance period	1450-1600
Baroque period	1600-1750
Classical period	1750-1825
Romantic period	1825-1900
Modern period	1900-present

Other elements that also affect style are: the group performing the music--jazz band, rock group, orchestra, et cetera; the individual composer's style, i.e. Johnny Cash, John Lennon, W.A. Mozart, et cetera; the performer's style, i.e. how the music is performed; the particular instrument used, a fine instrument or a cheap one; the nationality of the composer and the national orientation of the music, i.e. Anton Dvorak's "New World Symphony" (Dvorak is Czech, and the symphony is based on his experiences in visiting America); and the style the piece is written in, i.e. Beethoven might write a bombastic piece and also a light and lively piece. Thus, when we talk of style we might refer to Italian style, Beethovenish, operatic, singing style, jazzy, violin music, Country-Western, fiddle music, et cetera. As you listen to and discover various pieces of music during this course you will see many different elements that will affect the style of music.

Chapter VI: Glossary

form: the organizational aspects of a musical composition

repetition and contrast: the fundamental principles behind all musical form

symphonic form: structure of a large work for orchestra, comprised of several related movements

movements: distinct sections of larger musical works

strophic: each stanza of song uses same music

through-composed: new music is written for each verse of a song

binary form: two part form, i.e. AB or AABB

repeat sign: ||: :|| , means section enclosed in bars is repeated once

ternary form: three part form, i.e. ABA or AABA

alternating form: form where one main idea returns while alternating with other ideas, i.e. ABACA, ABACADA

sonata: a piece usually for solo instrument or solo instrument and piano, in three or four movements

sonata-allegro form, first movement form: a movement form comprising three major sections: exposition, development, and recapitulation

theme and variations: strict form where a theme is stated and then varied, i.e. A, A', A'', A''', et cetera

minuet and trio form: three part movement form, ABA, where the second A section is a da capo or exact repeat of the first minuet section

rondo form: an alternating form, i.e. ABACA, ABACADA

texture: relationship of the linear (melodic) and vertical (harmonic) aspects of music, three primary types: monophonic, polyphonic, homophonic

monophonic: "one sound", single melodic line

polyphonic: "many sounds", more than one melody going at the same time

homophonic: "same sound", melody with accompaniment

style: the distinguishing characteristics of a piece of music, affected by many elements: when and where composed, composer, performance medium, instruments, type of piece, et cetera

style periods: see page 77

Chapter VII

Attending Concerts and Recitals

One of the purposes of this course is to give you the background knowledge that will enable you to attend a concert of classical music with a better understanding of the whole sphere of music. This chapter is designed to present some of the typical concert situations, what you should expect, and how you should act in the concert hall.

The first thing you will discover on entering the concert hall will be that someone will hand you a program of the music to be performed. It is important to be able to decipher at least some of the hierogly-phics that are on a program so that you can understand what is about to happen. The following is a typical page from a program that you might be given if you attended a symphony concert.

PROGRAM

Overture to "The Magic Flute"................W. A. Mozart

Symphony #92 in G Major "Oxford"............F. J. Haydn
    Adagio—Allegro spiritoso
    Adagio
    Menuetto—Allegretto; Trio
    Presto

INTERMISSION

Jesu, Joy of Man's Desiring......J. S. Bach/arr. C. J. Roberts

An der schonen blauen Donau, Op. 314.......Johann Strauss

Finlandia, Op. 26, #7..........Jean Sibelius/arr. H. Sopkin

This particular page of the program tells what is to be performed. On the original program the front page indicated the group that was to perform, the director of the group, time, date, and place of the concert, and a picture of musical instruments. The next page consisted of the personnel in the performing group. (If it is a group from your home town or college, you may want to look through this section to see if you know someone who will be on stage.) Then the above page was the third page of the program.

Other items of pertinent information that you might find on subsequent pages of the program might be: a description of the pieces to be performed; a statement about the performers, the conductor, the composers and their music; and a translation of any songs that might be in a foreign language. All of these items are optional, but it pays to look through the entire program (turn it over, often there is something on the back!) as it may enlighten the experience you are about to have.

A detailed investigation of the above program will help you in understanding other programs you may see. The first work is "Overture to 'The Magic Flute'" by W.A. Mozart. You will learn that an overture is a short symphonic composition that usually precedes an opera and thus the music usually contains the main themes of the opera. In this case the opera is "The Magic Flute" by Mozart. You will not hear the opera, or any singing, only the instrumental prelude.

The second piece, "Symphony #92 in G Major 'Oxford'" by F.J. Haydn is a complete symphony, the 92nd that Haydn wrote. The key of the symphony is G major and the word "Oxford" is a sub-title that refers to when Haydn received an honorary degree from Oxford in 1791 where the symphony was performed. The indications below the symphony are the movements of the piece and the relative tempi (plural of tempo) of each. In this case there are four movements with the first movement having two tempi marked: Adagio--Allegro spiritoso, which means very slow (first section) and then fast, with spirit (second section). The second movement is Adagio, very slow. The third is marked Menuetto (minuet) and Trio (the form minuet and trio) and the tempo is allegretto, moderately fast. The last movement is a presto, very very fast. Each movement will probably seem to be a separate piece during the performance as there will usually be a short pause between each movement.

There follows an intermission, usually ten to fifteen minutes. This gives the orchestra and the audience a brief respite.

The second part of the program begins with a short work by J.S. Bach which was arranged for orchestra by C.J. Roberts. (An arrangement can take a variety of forms, usually a change in instrumentation.) In this case the piece "Jesu, Joy of Man's Desiring" was originally written for chorus and orchestra. Here it is performed by orchestra alone. Sometimes after a composer's name, the dates of the composer's birth and death will be given. This will give the audience a further indication of what style of music is about to be heard. Of course, if you know other works by the composer you will have a good idea of what is to come.

The title of the next work is written in German; the translation is "On the Beautiful Blue Danube" by Johann Strauss. Often, since pieces will be listed on programs in the language of the composer, it will be difficult to figure out the title unless you read the language. The Op, 314 (Opus means work) is an indication of when the piece was written or published in the chronological order of the composer's works. This would seem to indicate that it was the three hundred and fourteenth piece that J. Strauss wrote, but since it could refer to the publication date or order instead of the time it was written the opus number can be somewhat deceiving. However you could assume that this is, indeed, a mature work of Johann Strauss. In the case of Johann Sebastian Bach's works (Bach had three sons who were also important musicians) the chronological order of his works is listed by BMV numbers, i.e. BMV 609; in Mozart's works by Kochel or K. numbers, i.e. K. 251; and in Schubert's works by Deutsche or D. numbers, i.e. D. 122.

The final piece on the program is a piece called "Finlandia" written by the Finnish composer Jean Sibelius, and here arranged by H. Sopkin. (In this arrangement the chorus is omitted by the arranger and more instruments added.)

After studying the program you might take notice of the atmosphere of the concert hall. Most classical music lovers seem to be rather sedate and sophisticated to the uninitiated concert goer. This formality is an inherent part of a classical performance and part of going to a recital is learning the appropriate etiquette.

First of all it is important to sit quietly while the performer (s) are on stage, whether the performance is in progress or not. A certain respect should be given to the performers who will undoubtedly be very nervous about the experience; distracting noises and talking can be very disturbing to the performers' composure and concentration. It is VERY INappropriate to eat, drink, or chew gum at a concert. So for the performers' benefit do not talk, whisper, rattle papers about, or bring popcorn to a recital. It is important to realize that you may also be disturbing some of the other members of the audience, the classical music lovers, and they probably outnumber you considerably. (Do not push an irate classival music lover! Bad things could happen!!!)

It is also not appropriate to enter or leave an auditorium during a performance. Always wait until there is a major pause between pieces or movements. (Emergencies are the exception, but being bored is NOT an emergency.)

Performers like to receive applause, but during a classical performance it is only proper to applaud after each complete piece, not after each section or movement of a piece. Great performances may be further accoladed by shouting bravo. Whistling is not generally appropriate, though some of us will take what we can get.

It is basic concert etiquette to respect the performers. Remember that it is his/her/their moment on stage, and it is usually pretty difficult for them.

Many programs of classical music are different from the one detailed above. Band concerts will be different from orchestra concerts, and each type of recital will differ from another. Thus chamber recitals, violin recitals, piano recitals, voice recitals will all specialize in certain areas of classical music. There are also mixed recitals where a variety of performers will take part. All of this can add to the interest of the program and you may find you really like one type of program and dislike another. The experience is yours to make something important out of it.

PART II

Music History

Introduction

A brief and very broad overview of music history
can give the non-music student a much deeper understanding of how certain forms and styles of music, with which
he is perhaps unfamiliar, developed, and also give him
an appreciation for the many types of music that people
enjoy. This historical progression can also give a background understanding of the music that he does listen
to and appreciate. Western music has had a remarkable
development of many diverse styles over long centuries
of turbulent history. It is important for the student
to remember that the musical heritage of a particular
era is closely allied to the momentous historical
happenings and social conditions of the time. The music
will have more meaning if the student keeps this in
mind throughout this section of the course.

This text will trace music history from Greek times
(approximately 600 B.C.) through modern Classical music.
This progression will, as already stated, be very broad
with the emphasis on major changes in musical styles.
Listening examples for the music of various periods
will be played in class, and through lectures, recordings, and experiences you should receive a good basic
understanding of Western music history. In this general
overview many forms, styles, and composers must be left
out, but, as much as possible, a continuous line of
development will be presented throughout this section.

Chapter I

Greek Heritage

It is difficult to pinpoint the exact influences that Greek music heritage have had on Western music history, but there can be little doubt that our music has been profoundly affected by this tradition. Most of our knowledge of Greek music comes from manuscripts that discuss the music rather than from actual pieces of music. This provides us with a great deal of information about the music but little practical knowledge of what the music may have sounded like.

One of the important aspects of Greek music was a philosophy called the Doctrine of Ethos. The Greeks felt that music was not passive but rather that it actively affected a man. The morality and temperament of a person would be directly affected by the type of music he heard. (A concept we would all be wise to consider, perhaps.) Thus, if I listen to music that evokes strong passions (anger, conflict), I might be affected by the music in a violent manner. The Greeks felt so strongly about this that it was thought to be very important to educate a man with just the right balance of different types of music, so that his character would be appropriate for his tasks in life.

Music played an important role in the Greek religion. The cult of Apollo was associated with the soothing, calming music of the lyre and kithara (string instruments, vaguely similar to but smaller than the modern harp, which were plucked). The cult of Dyonysus was associated with stronger emotions and an instrument called the aulos (a double-pipe reed instrument with a sharp, shrill tone.

Greek music was also associated with drama and poetry and was basically improvisatory in performance practices. The music was rhythmically closely allied to the rhythm and meter of poetry, prose, and dance. It was primarily monophonic, perhaps with notes added by the instrumentalist to "embellish" the melody.

Greek music theory was based on a system of eight modes (similar to scales). We can only guess what these scales sounded like, but from treatises we can assume that the Greeks used a wide variety of microtones (intervals smaller than a half step) and that the scales differed greatly from those we use today. These modes were also an important part of the Ethos or effect of a particular piece on a person's character, each mode, combined with other aspects of the music, having a different effect.

The Greek musical system was scientifically based on acoustical principles that are still valid today. Pythagoras measured the vibrating lengths of strings in the 6th century B.C. and determined the proportions of the string with respect to the various intervals, i.e. octave 1:2 (double the length of the string and the sound will be one octave lower, et cetera, see page 60, the overtone series).

The whole concept of Greek music was interwoven into Greek life. From religion to astronomy and mathematics the Greeks were concerned with the totality of the musical experience. How much of this knowledge has transferred into Western musical theory and practice is difficult to comprehend fully, but we can appreciate the profound involvement that music played in Greek life.

Chapter I: Glossary

Doctrine of Ethos: Doctrine or philosophy dealing with the moral effects of music on a person's character

lyre and kithara: string instruments similar to the harp but smaller, associated with the Apollonian cult

Apollonian cult: music associated with the God Apollo-- soothing, calm

Dionysian cult: music associated with the God Dionysus-- strong emotions, passions

aulos: double-pipe reed instrument with shrill, piercing tone, associated with Dionysian cult

Greek music: associated with drama, poetry, and dance; monophonic; improvisatory; use of Greek modes

Greek modes: system of eight scales used in Greek music

Chapter II

Medieval Period: 400-1450

The Middle Ages or Dark Ages is the period immediately following the disintegration of the Roman Empire. The majority of the populace were destitute peasants under the thumbs of feudal lords. Communications
and travel were minimal: peasants left the farm only
to help fight petty wars for their masters or to go to
church. The Church of the Medieval period was the only
unifying factor in this crude culture. Catholicism grew
in strength throughout the early Middle Ages giving the
people a purpose for their hard and often cruel life.
The Church, Catholicism, was the neutral ground where
God could be petitioned and hope could be given to the
destitute for their salvation and a better life in the
hereafter.

The Catholic Churches were also the only true centers of artistic growth. Traveling monks and priests
shared ideas and the faith in songs throughout early
Medieval Europe. It is in the Church of this period that
we study early art and music. What we know of music
theory and musical practice comes almost exclusively
from monastic centers, this knowledge having been passed
down through hundreds of years by word of mouth, or
later by transcriptions.

We will study the Medieval period in several sections. The first will be concerned with the music of the
early Church: approximately 400-1000 A.D. The second
section will deal with early secular music, 11th through
13th centuries. The third part will deal with the development of early polyphony and the revival of economic
growth and intercity travel, 10th through 13th centuries. The last section, called the "Ars Nova" or "New
Art", will discuss the expansion of polyphony and movement toward the Renaissance in the arts and in philosophy, 14th and early 15th centuries.

All of these sections will center on the music and
influence of the Catholic Church (Roman and Greek Ortho-
dox--though after mid-15th century and the fall of
Constantinople, Eastern influences are minimal). Most
of this music will seem very simple and strange since
you rarely come into contact with it in your daily
lives. The musical theory or structure is different
from the music you listen to today, but it is the heritage from which the system of major/minor tonality

eventually grew.

Music of the Early Church: to 1000 A.D.

It is impossible to tell how the music of Greek Culture eventually influenced the music of the early Church. With the fall of the Roman Empire, the Catholic Church systematically destroyed the "pagan" practices of Roman rites and music. Very little information is available to make the connection from Greek music through Roman practice to the Catholic Church, which was the primary influence on the arts until the Renaissance.

Music of the early Church (Church is capitalized here to refer to the Roman Catholic Church) was similar to the hymns and chanting found at that time in Jewish services and the chanting in eastern (Byzantine) services. The Church in Byzantium (Constantinople, presently Istanbul) had a strong initial influence on early Roman Catholic music.

Because of the difficulty of travel and communications in the early Medieval period, different services and music developed in various parts of Europe. Besides the Byzantine and Roman Churches, other centers of chant included: Gallican--France, Mozarabic--Spain, Ambrosian--Milan, Italy, and Sarum--England. Each of these areas were influenced by local practices and various outside influences.

One of the difficulties in studying early Church music stems from the fact it was not until the 11th century that chants began to be written down. Until that time they were passed down from generation to generation of monks and priests in the monasteries. What changes evolved during this time are not known, though it is remarkable to note the similarities between chants from different regions once they began to be notated.

Gregorian Chant

The center of the Catholic Church was at Rome and the Roman Rites and liturgy eventually came to dominate the music of Europe. In the 6th century A.D. Pope Gregory I (The Great) began the task of organizing and standardizing the liturgy and chants of the Church. Though it is doubtful whether he wrote any of the chants, they have become known as Gregorian chant.

Gregorian chant, plain chant, plainsong, or cantus plainus, is the large body of Church music that was established as the official music of the Roman Catholic Church. Chanting was an ideal form of _functional_ music for the purposes of the Church. Functional music means music that serves a specific purpose, in this case worship of God. The chants were sung to help put the worshippers into the appropriate mood for praising God. This is an important consideration when listening to the music of the early Church. It was not supposed to be exciting.

Gregorian chant is monophonic, has no definite rhythm, a narrow melodic range, and predominantly step-wise motion. It was composed of short melodic motives that were "strung together" to form the chant. From these practices a system of theory of music was eventually derived.

Music of this period is built from eight modes, Church modes, or scales, that are different from the Greek modes. These scales are patterns of whole and half steps, but with patterns that are different from those of major/minor tonality. They do use eight notes in the octave. From this very early scale system, derived from long-sustained connecting motives, the major/minor system eventually developed. The complete form of the modes was not reached until the 11th century.

Gregorian chant is originally improvisatory in character and has no definite rhythm. This gives the chant a feeling of continuous development and movement very conducive to a calm, subdued atmosphere for worship. The rhythm was based on the natural rhythms of the texts.

The language of the Church and of Gregorian chant is Latin. The chants use primarily Biblical texts, particularly from the Psalms. The most important service of the Catholic Church is the Mass, and since we will be listening to and studying this form throughout more than a thousand years of music history, it is important to know the major sections of the Mass that are set to music: Kyrie (_Lord_ have mercy), Gloria (_Glory_ to God in the Highest), Credo (_Creed_, I believe in one God), Sanctus--Benedictus (_Holy_, holy, holy--_Blessed_), Agnus Dei (_Lamb of God_).

In performance the chants were sung a cappella (no instrumental accompaniment) and by men's voices in the monasteries and churches. The primary methods of performance were: <u>responsorial</u>--leader sings, choir or congregation responds or repeats; <u>antiphonal</u>-- one group, choir, follows or answers another; and <u>direct</u>--everyone together. The chants were sung (set to music) either syllabically, neumatically, or melismatically: <u>syllabic</u> means one note to a syllable; <u>neumatic</u>, a few (2 to 5) notes to a syllable; and <u>melismatic</u>, many notes to a syllable. There was also the use of a <u>reciting tone</u>: a long string of syllables were sung on one note which changed only at the end of the phrase.

[Example of Gregorian chant in modern notation: notation of rhythm and pitch are only approximate as often the neumes (old form of notation) are simply representations of approximate pitch and rhythm.]

The original Gregorian chants were later modified by the addition of melismatic passages to some syllables and eventually by the addition of words. This was called <u>troping</u> and is the first development toward adding musical interest to the chants. A special kind of trope was created by adding words and music to the word "alleluia". These were called <u>sequences</u>.

The effect of the music of the early Church can only be reflected in the conditions of the time. A peasant going to church in the Dark Ages would be entering a cold, damp, dark, and often smelly building to spend a few moments away from the hardship of his life. Here he could lose himself in the worship of his God. The strong superstitions of this age led the peasants to place their whole trust and welfare in the keeping of the Church. This brief respite for the church-goer of that time would be a nightmare to us. His beliefs gave him the inner strength to continue for another week. The heavy incense, used to help cover up the smells of the unwashed populace and damp conditions, plus the heavy calming music, seemingly added to the mysteries and effects of faith.

Early Secular Music

The earliest examples of secular or popular music, dating from the 11th century, were called Goliard songs. (We must assume that popular forms of music were in existence before this, but we do not have any examples.) Goliards were wandering, ne'er do well, students who went from monastic school to school. The music was similar to Gregorian chant in style: monophonic, narrow range, Latin texts; however, the content of the texts were often far from religious. The favorite topics being love, humor, and drink--does that sound familiar?

The wandering musician was the mainstay of Medieval popular music, and the period from the 11th through 13th centuries saw a wide variety of these musicians, composers and their songs. Some, like the minstrels and jongleurs, were of the lower classes and lived as outcasts moving from village to village doing tricks, acrobatics, plays, and musical performances. Others were from higher classes and often composed their own music: troubadours, trouveres, and minnesingers.

The music of these wandering musicians was very similar to Gregorian chant from which many melodies were derived. It must be remembered that the profound influence of the Catholic Church was felt in all areas of life in the Middle Ages and that the popular music would necessarily reflect the many long years the people were exposed to chant in church.

The music was typically of narrow range, mono-phonic, step-wise motion, modal (use of modes), and was sung either to no set rhythm, to dance rhythms, or to the rhythmic patterns of the words of the texts. The texts ranged from non-liturgical religious texts to bawdy love and drinking songs. The main language was the Latin of the Church, but this practice slowly changed and the texts appeared more and more in the vernacular (native language of the region).

Two types of songs from this period are the chanson de geste, an epic poem set to music, emulating knightly deeds and heroes of feudal Europe, and the pastourelle, a dramatic ballad that tells a simple story. The pastourelle was usually a love story in a pastoral setting (the shepherdess, her lover, and the evil knight; or a variation on this theme). It was composed of a number of syllabic songs put together to tell a story. In a sense it was the first form of opera.

The most famous pastourelle is "Jeu de Robin et Marion" or "Games of Robin and Marion" (not Robin Hood and Maid Marion) written in the late 13th century by Adam de la Halle, a famous trouvere.

The primary musical style of the Middle Ages was vocal. Instrumental music is almost always associated with either vocal music or as an accompaniment to dances. Initially this was simply playing the melodies in unison or octaves and perhaps occasionally adding notes to the melody or "embellishing" it. The instruments were very crude, not standardized in size or shape, and often one played whatever was on hand at the time.

Some of the popular instruments of the period were: psaltery--string instrument similar to a zither that was plucked; vielle--bowed string instrument and the very early predecessor of the violin; hurdy-gurdy-- another string instrument that was played by turning a crank that was attached to a wheel that stroked the strings; harp; flutes--both the recorder, a wooden flute held in front of the performer, and the transverse flute, similar to today's instrument; shawms--double reed instruments with a piercing tone; various sizes and shapes of trumpets and horns; drums; the organ-- played by man-powered bellows; and bagpipes--a very popular instrument in Europe.

Rise of Polyphony

During the later developments in Gregorian chant a slow development of an important new texture began. Polyphony, or the use of more than one independent line of music first appeared in about the 10th century A.D. The original form of polyphonic music was very simple, only a small step from singing a melody in octaves. Parallel organum or simple organum was the doubling of a chant at the interval of a fourth or fifth above or below the original chant.

Parallel Organum

In another form of simple organum, the voices started at the unison and then moved to the interval of a fourth, proceeded in parallel motion, and then cadenced by returning to the unison:

Glo ri a in ex cel sis De o

   While these forms are very simple, an important
development in music derived from this new texture. The
use of different melodic lines made the concept of a
musical notation much more important, so it is from
this period that we begin to see the first forms of
notation. Initially musical notation was restricted to
pitch and was very simple. The first extant examples
are simply markings above the text with eventually a
one line "staff" inserted to give added approximation
of pitch above and below the line. The neumes (notes--
early form of notation) were marks, what we might refer
to as "chicken scratches", made at varying heights above
the text or line (10th-11th centuries). Later more lines
were added and the neumes became more distinct. By the
12th and 13th centuries there were three and four line
staffs which indicated fairly accurately the pitch. It
was not until the 14th century that the five note staff
was generally used. The increasing accuracy of notational systems parallels the increasing complexity of polyphony and the resulting need for better notation. Of
course, the advent of notation also has important historical significance as the first examples of the music
of Western culture were preserved.

   The next development in polyphony was in the use
of motion in the melodic lines that was not parallel:
oblique motion--where one line remains on the same
note and the other line moves; and contrary motion--
where the lines move in opposite directions.

      oblique motion   contrary motion

   An important aspect of polyphony is the use of an
original Gregorian chant as the primary melody. This
practice lasted for many centuries in a variety of
forms. The original chant line became known as the

95

<u>cantus</u> <u>firmus</u>, or "firm song".

In the 12th century a new type of organum appears, called St. Martial organum or "florid" organum. Here the original Gregorian melody or cantus firmus is sustained in longer note values and the added melody is melismatic and freer rhythmically. (Upper voice moves in faster note values to the lower voice, or cantus firmus.)

With the rise of independent rhythmic parts the existing notation proved to be inadequate so a new form of notation was developed to help indicate various rhythmic patterns. A system of <u>rhythmic</u> <u>modes</u> or patterns of rhythms was used, and at the beginning of a piece it was indicated which of these modes was to be used.

Rhythmic modes

From these early beginnings polyphonic music grew rapidly and acquired new complexities and rhythmic freedom in the different voices. Much of the music was liturgical and still in Latin, but polyphony soon began to be used in secular songs. The music expanded to three and then four voices moving at the same time. Latin and vernacular texts were used together, and eventually sacred and popular texts were also mixed. In fact, the cantus firmus line became so long and sustained that it was no longer an identifiable melody and was only used as a unifying device in the music. By the end of the 13th century the rhythm became freer and rhythmic notation also improved.

The social climate expanded throughout this period with the renewal of travel and trade between towns, cities, and countries. The new era was ushered in, first by the sturdy, solid Romanesque architecture in the 12th century, and then by the elaborate Gothic architecture of the 13th. Humanity was beginning to find itself, and the growth of art, music, and literature continued to gain momentum. The Catholic Church found the new freedom of man slowly undermining its stranglehold on the

arts. However, it was not until the Renaissance that
man fully flowered as an individual.

The Ars Nova, The New Art: 14th-early 15th
Century, Toward the Renaissance

In the 14th century the power of the Catholic
Church was seriously questioned for the first time. Man
began to believe that reason and revelation should be
separate: that the Church and State had separate
responsibilities; the Church was responsible for the
soul, while the State was responsible for earthly concerns. The corrupt life-styles of some of the higher
clergy in the Church led to a questioning of the
Church's power. During this period the Papacy and
Church had their own troubled inner concerns. At one
point during the 14th century, for example, there were
three different popes at one time, and from 1305-1378
the popes were in exile in France.

The plague, or Black Death, ravaged Europe from
1348-1350 and the One Hundred Years War also took its
toll. As Europe came under the rule of the absolute
monarchies and kings began to defy the Church, the
feudal system collapsed.

The main difference between the music of the 12th
and 13th centuries, the Ars Antiqua or Old Art, and the
music of the 14th century or Ars Nova was the increase
in rhythmic complexity and freedom. The leading composer
in France during the Ars Nova was Guillaume de Machaut
(1300-1377). His music uses more secular texts, is
generally longer, and has much greater complexity in
the rhythm than that of previous composers. He also
uses a rhythmic device popular at this time called
isorhythm (same-rhythm). This is where a set pattern of
intervals (pitches) and another pattern of rhythms are
repeated throughout a piece in one voice as a unifying
device. Later several or all of the voices might be
written in isorhythms.

One of Machaut's important contributions was the
writing of a Mass ("Messe de Notre Dame" or "Mass of
Our Lady") as a complete unit. Until this time (and
actually for some time to come) each section of the
Mass (Kyrie, Gloria, et cetera) was composed separately,
unrelated in style to other parts. Different sections
were often taken from the works of various composers
for a service. However, the "Messe de Notre Dame" was
conceived as a whole, related in mood and style, and

97

was thus expected to be kept intact for a service. This eventually (in about seventy years) led to much greater unity in the various parts of the Mass.

Popular music also developed rapidly within the new found rhythmic freedom. Forms such as the Ballade, Rondeau, and Medieval Madrigal became popular. The Medieval madrigal was a polyphonic composition for two voices with pastoral, romantic, and satirical texts, often with several stanzas that were sung to the same music (strophic).

At the beginning of the 15th century, at the court of the Dukes of Burgundy in northern France, a "School" of music emerged as the dominant trend. The courts as well as the churches now began to be important centers of art and music. Two composers emerged as leaders of this style: Guillaume Dufay (1400-1474) and Gilles Binchois (1400-1460).

One of the important developments of the Burgundian school was the unified settings of the Mass using one melody (cantus firmus) as the basis for all the movements (sections of the Mass). This use of Gregorian melodies as a unifying device in a large composition continued throughout this period and the next.

Another very important development was the slow change from the use of fourths and fifths as consonant intervals to the use of thirds and sixths. This practice originally used in England eventually came to into common practice on the continent. This gradual change over is the first real movement toward major/minor tonality with the use of harmony built on thirds. With the added use of the raised seventh scale degree in some of the modes leaning toward our major and minor scale patterns, the music begins to take on some of the shape and sound that we are used to hearing. The use of definite cadences (or chord progressions that reach a point of rest) of varying types helps to accent the feeling of a harmonic or vertical language within the polyphonic writing, and more frequent use of homorhythmic style (each part moves in parallel rhythms) is used in a variety of forms. However, the music is still linearly based and it is still some time before we see the true use of chords and chordal relationships.

The music of the Ars Nova and Burgundian school became more complex and interesting through these developments. The Church, however, saw this complexity and freedom as a threat to the atmosphere of worship. The turmoil between the Church and State reach a climax musically in the next period, but it is important to remember the powerful influence that the Church still had upon music and art during the entire Medieval period. Even the secular music was still strongly influenced by what was written in the religious sphere.

Chapter II: Glossary

Roman Catholic Church: Main religion of Europe during Middle Ages, Rome was center of Catholic faith, chants of the Roman liturgy eventually codified other forms into one main liturgy

Gregorian chant: chants of the early Church collected and standardized into Roman liturgy by Pope Gregory I

plain chant, plain song, cantus planus: Gregorian chant, monophonic, functional music, indefinite rhythm, composed of short melodic motives "strung together", originally improvisatory in style, narrow melodic range, stepwise motion, sung unaccompanied

Church modes: eight modes (scales) formulated from early Medieval chanting practices; eight notes in the octave with varying half and whole step patterns

Latin: language of the Church and Gregorian chants

Mass: main Catholic service, comprised of five major sections that were set to music: Kyrie, Gloria, Credo, Sanctus-Benedictus, Agnus Dei

a cappella: not accompanied, voices without accompaniment

Ways Gregorian chant was sung:

> responsorial: leader sings, choir or congregation follows

> antiphonal: one group or choir answers another

> direct: unison, everyone sings together

Ways Catholic liturgy was set to music of chants:

syllabic: one note to a syllable

neumatic: two to five notes to a syllable

melismatic: many notes to a syllable

reciting tone: many syllables recited to a single note that does not change pitch until the phrase of the text is finished, at which point it might raise or lower a step

goliards, minstrels, and jongleurs: lower class wandering musicians of the Middle Ages

troubadours, trouveres, minnesingers: higher class students, composers, who were wandering musicians

vernacular: local, native language, i.e. French in France

chanson de geste: secular song, epic poem about heroic deeds set to music

pastourelle: dramatic ballad composed of short songs strung together to tell a story, nature, love plot and setting

"Jeu de Robin et Marion": pastourelle by Adam de la Halle

Adam de la Halle: famous trouvere (circa 13th century)

embellishing, ornamentation: adding notes to already existing melody as a coloristic effect

instruments of the Medieval period: see page 94

parallel organum, simple organum: first form of polyphony, two lines of music, original chant doubled at the interval of a fourth or fifth below

oblique motion: motion of voice parts in polyphony where one voice remains on the same note and other voice moves

contrary motion: motion in polyphony where voices move in opposite directions

cantus firmus: use of Gregorian chant melody as one of the lines of polyphony; continues through 16th century; literally "firm song"

St. Martial organum, florid organum: sustained cantus firmus with melismatic chant or melody set above

rhythmic modes: early form of rhythmic notation--set specific rhythmic patterns in the music, came into use because of the need for more definite rhythmic notation in chants where the parts no longer coincided rhythmically (as in St. Martial organum)

Ars Nova: "New Art" of the 14th century, distinguished from the "Ars Antiqua" of the 13th century by increased rhythmic freedom and complexity

Guillaume de Machaut: (1300-1377) leading composer of the Ars Nova

Burgundian school: early 15th century group of composers at the court of the Dukes of Burgundy in northern France, two important composers were Guillaume Dufay (1400-1474) and Gilles Binchois (1400-1460)

tropes, troping: addition of words and music to original chants, a special type of trope set to the word "alleluia" was called the sequence

neumes: early form of notation

isorhythm: "same-rhythm", popular device of 14th century where a set interval pattern and set rhythm pattern would be repeated throughout a piece in one or more of the voices as a unifying device

homorhythmic texture: each voice part moves in parallel rhythms, leaning toward homophonic texture, but music is still organized as separate melodies or polyphonically

Chapter III

The Renaissance: 1450-1600

The age of the Renaissance was marked by man's awakening to a sense of his own importance. The dominance of the divine order had begun to give way to the importance of secular affairs. Man had begun to believe in himself and his abilities. Reason replaced faith and man now had a sense of his own power and beauty. It was the time of da Vinci, Michelangelo, Shakespeare, Luther, and in music, Palestrina and Des Prez. The Renaissance man had a new love of art and beauty that was realistic, sensuous, simplistic, and embued with nature. Exploration and adventure, as well as the beginning of science and invention, sparked the new fever of man's development. Compared to this the past era was indeed the "Dark Ages."

The music of the Renaissance saw the growth of polyphony reach its height in the music of the Catholic Church. Despite the new music of the Reformation (1517) and the continued loss of power over cultural affairs the Catholic Church still wielded enough power to influence the greatest composers of the period. However, music continued to grow in many ways and new forms and developments leaned ever closer to the transformation into major/minor tonality.

Polyphonic music took on an even more complicated form in the Renaissance. The texture of the vocal music began typically to use four or more parts that functioned equally in a linear sense. This obviously added to the complexity of the music and the difficulty of notation and performance.

Counterpoint is a term that is virtually synonymous in meaning to polyphony, but it tends to be used to indicate a type of polyphony that is somewhat stricter in style. During the Renaissance the interweaving of the four voice parts took on a more imitative function. Imitative counterpoint is where one line actually imitates another line at the same pitch or begins at another pitch and then maintains the same melodic pattern. This "imitation" does not have to be exact and often it is not, but it is another form of unifying device used extensively by Renaissance composers. A composition in very strict imitation is called a canon (not cannon, i.e. the weapon).

103

Below is an example of a canon in two parts.

(Top voice starts one measure later at the interval of
a fifth above the lower voice in very strict imitation.)

With the development of more and more complicated
interwoven voice parts the bass or lower voice began to
take on a more harmonic function, especially in movement toward cadences. The Renaissance composers were
very concerned with the vertical element of music in
the sense of the intervals (preference of thirds,
sixths, and octaves as consonant intervals) NOT in the
sense of chords or chord progressions. The fundamental
orientation was still toward the melodic lines and
their relationship to each other. So even though the
intervals of thirds and sixths were consonant (the
basic building blocks of major/minor tonality) and the
bass attained a more harmonic function, the music of
the Renaissance remained polyphonic in style and texture. The paths had now been paved for the advent of
major/minor tonality, but a change in emphasis from
melody to harmony was needed for the final transition.

The early Renaissance composers (important ones
are Johannes Ockeghem, ca. 1420-1494, and Josquin
Des Prez, 1450-1521) also used Gregorian chants as the
basis for many of their compositions. However the
cantus firmus began to be used very freely, often being
elongated beyond recognition or changed in other ways.
It also became popular to use secular tunes as the
basis for religious compositions like Masses. Eventually the Catholic Church reacted very strongly against
the complexity of music in general and the practices
of secularizing Church music with popular idioms.
Catholic music of the late Renaissance reflected the
reaction of composers to the ire of the Church by
returning to a more functional music for worship.

Secular Vocal Music

During the Renaissance popular music became even

more important than it had been before and many new forms developed. Almost all the composers of this period, including the serious Church composers, put their hands to writing light cheerful tunes for the public.

Perhaps the most famous form of popular music that emerged was the Italian madrigal. Basically a poem set to music, this was a light, generally four (or five) part vocal piece that used texts about love, nature, and political farce. With the relaxation of the Church's stranglehold on music and the arts, and the awakening of interest in the individual man, humanity almost overreacted in its attempt at humor in music. Many of the madrigal texts are very bawdy and in some instances even crass in nature. They also abound in double meanings. Below are two typical madrigal texts:

My dear lady,
I want to sing
A song under your window
With my lance as my companion.
Don, diridon

(Excerpt from an Italian madrigal by Orlando di Lasso)

Lady if you spight me,
Wherefore do you so often kiss and delight me?
Sure that my heart oppressed and overcloyed,
May break thus overjoyed.
If you seek to spill me.
Come kiss me sweet and kill me.
So that your heart be eased,
And I shall rest content and die well pleased.

(English madrigal by John Dowland)

A popular device of the madrigal and many of the vocal pieces of this period was the use of word painting. Word painting occurs when the composer attempts to "paint" a word or words of the text of a song with the musical line. For instance, the music rises on the word heaven, lowers on the word hell; or as another example, mimics the familiar cuckoo of the cuckoo bird.

The texture of the madrigal is polyphonic, sometimes strictly contrapuntal, but often very "chordal"
or homorhythmic in character. Italian madrigals, English
madrigals, and other popular four and five part songs
of the Renaissance that were influenced by the Italian
madrigal (French, chanson; German, lied; English, Ayre)
can be either strophic, or more often through-composed,
and some forms have a refrain (a part that is repeated
after each verse--an English favorite is something like
Fa-la-la-la-la). Often these pieces were accompanied by
instruments--one of the most popluar being the lute (a
predecessor to the guitar).

Instrumental Music

For the first time instrumental music begins to
establish itself as a separate entity from vocal music.
Even though most of the instrumental forms can be traced
back to older vocal forms, music was now being written
specifically for instruments. The most popular forms
and styles of instrumental pieces are those related to
dances of the period.

The instruments themselves began to improve and
standardize to a certain extent. Still, the compositions
did not specify, until the very end of the Renaissance,
what instruments were to be used on what part. Invari-
ably, the performers used whatever instruments were
available: higher instruments on the treble parts and
lower instruments on the bass parts.

Instruments of the Renaissance

Double reeds: shawms, bombards (bass shawms), curtals
(early bassoons)

"Brass": cornetts (made of wood and ivory and shaped
much differently from today's instruments), sackbut
(early trombone), and many other forms

Strings: viol family (instruments of varying sizes that
approximate the modern violin family--the major differences are that the viols have flat backs, resonate less
than the modern violins, and use frets), tromba marina
(long box-shaped instrument with one bowed string and
many "sympathetic" strings inside the box that vibrated
in sympathy with the notes played)

Organs: rapid development; very large pipe organs whose
bellows were operated by teams of men jumping up and

down on them

Clavichord: early keyboard instrument whose strings were set in motion by a being struck by a metal tangent

Harpsichord: popular keyboard instrument whose strings are set in motion by a quill that plucks the string (also called the virginal, clavicin)

Lute: most popular instrument of the Renaissance, plucked and strummed like a guitar; it had a pear-shaped body (an early form of the guitar appeared in Spain called the vihuela)

Instrumental music of the Renaissance was largely improvisatory in style. This means that the pieces were free stylistically and often had the feeling of being made up during the performance (and probably occasionally were). Keyboard music, especially, developed the improvisatory style, while other compositions often sounded that way because of added notes or embellishments from the performer. The variation form was particularly applicable to improvisation where the melody was freely varied.

Late Renaissance Catholic Music

With the Reformation and the beginning of important independent secular vocal and instrumental forms of music, the Church began to lose its influence on the musical arts. From 1543 to 1563 the Catholic Church held a Council at Trent at which two of the important considerations were the revision of existing music to fit the Church's idea of functional, reverent music and the admonishment of contemporary composers to respect the forms of sacred music. The result of this council was to have a profound effect on some of the important late Renaissance Catholic composers. While the Church did not dictate exactly what the composer should compose, it advised that the music needed to be less secular in orientation and more religious or functional in style.

While the composers could have simply taken a great step back to the Middle Ages and composed music similar to that which had been composed before, what actually happened was a triumph for polyphony and imitative counterpoint.

Giovanni Pierluigi da Palestrina (1525-1594) or

simply, Palestrina, took the difficult, complex elements
of linear imitative polyphony and, within the guidelines
established by the Church, wrote exquisite, awe-inspir-
ing music. His music is so important in the development
of music history and theory that whole courses of 16th
century counterpoint are taught (often two semesters in
length) to music majors, based on his style. His genius
and real gift to music was that he was able to take a
then popular form of composition (imitative counterpoint), bring it to its height in complexity and style
and, at the same time, return the music to the functional desires of the Church, while adding the depth and
beauty of a great creative mind.

To understand Palestrina's counterpoint you would
have to study very assiduously for many years, but
basically, he used a variety of imitative techniques to
achieve an interweaving of melodic lines that has not
since been equaled. It took an incredible genius to
build the complex relationships of melodic, linear,
harmonic, and intervalic sonority into an expressive
masterwork.

Sixteenth century counterpoint studied today is
approached by books of complicated "rules" that explain
and illustrate the complex music that Palestrina wrote
naturally. Some of these basic techniques of imitative
counterpoint, when examined briefly, can give an understanding of the complexity of the music. Not only could
a melody be imitated (as seen before on page 104)
strictly by another voice, either on the same note
starting at a different time, or following the same
pattern starting on a different note, but it could also
be varied by several other techniques: diminution,
meaning that the imitating part would be in smaller
note values,

(Lower voice in diminution at the unison)

108

augmentation, meaning the imitating part would be longer
note values (augmented)

(Lower voice in augmentation at the fourth below)

retrograde, meaning that the imitative part would be
done backwards,

(Upper voice in retrograde at the unison. This
means that the composer would have to have the ending
of the piece in mind while he wrote the beginning.)

and inversion, referring to turning the melody "upside
down".

(Lower voice is an inversion at the octave.)

All of these techniques could also be combined, i.e.
retrograde-diminution (backwards and in smaller note

109

values), which made the process even more complicated.

If you can imagine the complexity of a composition of four parts that used a combination of these techniques in all the voices and yet had to stay within the strict standards of the vertical and linear sound combinations of the period, you would begin to begin to see how difficult this whole process could be. AND during Palestrina's life time he and other composers wrote compositions using as many as twelve or more parts in imitative counterpoint, all interweaving according to very specific techniques and guidelines.

Beyond that it is simply very pleasurable to listen to Palestrina's music. It has a calm, soothing, serene affect and a "celestial" beauty. The lines move in and out in a continuous unfolding and mixing of melody; the rhythm of Renaissance music is more measured (sense of a steady beat) than earlier music, but the continuous flow of contrapuntal music is achieved by the overlapping of cadences. Another important composer from this period who also exhibits Palestrina's wonderful grace and style is Orlando di Lasso, or di Lasso.

Toward the Baroque

The music of the late Renaissance progressed steadily toward the harmonic, rhythmic, and tonal relationships that led to major/minor tonality and homophonic texture. Raised leading tones (seventh scale degrees), use of a harmonically functioning bass part, increased awareness of the vertical element of music within the linear aspect of polyphony, and the increasing use of instrumental accompaniments to secular vocal music all contributed to the trend that finally gave birth to the next period. The Renaissance had set the stage for a new era of growth in music and the arts. Inventions, exploration, and man's faith in his own abilities led to a renewed artistic growth that continued throughout the Western world. The Baroque period took the gifts of the Renaissance and translated them into a new musical style. It was the advent of major/minor tonality, homophony, and a new era.

Chapter III: Glossary

Renaissance: 1450-1600, period marked by man's awakening, reason replaced faith, man believed in his own
abilities

counterpoint: term virtually synonymous with polyphony

imitative counterpoint: strict counterpoint where the
original melody is imitated either directly or slightly
changed, this can include a variety of contrapuntal
techniques (see pages 108-109)

contrapuntal: referring to counterpoint

early Renaissance composers: Johannes Ockeghem (ca.
1420-1495) and Josquin Des Prez (1450-1521)

canon: a direct form of imitative counterpoint, very
strict imitation

Italian madrigal: poem set to music; popular song of
the Renaissance; typically four or five part setting;
nature, love, political satire plots; polyphonic or
homorhythmic; strophic or through-composed

word painting: "painting" words in musical line, i.e.
word, "heaven", music moves up

refrain: repeated sections after each verse

instruments of the Renaissance: see pages 106-107

improvisatory: having the quality and freedom of
improvisation, i.e. making it up as you go along

Palestrina: (1525-1594), famous Catholic Church composer of imitative polyphony

di Lasso (1532-1594), composer, contemporary of
Palestrina

<u>contrapuntal</u> <u>techniques</u>:

<u>augmentation</u>: original melody imitated with longer note values

<u>diminution</u>: original melody imitated with shorter note values

<u>retrograde</u>: original melody imitated backwards

<u>inversion</u>: original melody imitated by inverting it

Chapter IV

The Baroque Period: 1600-1750

The tern Baroque probably comes from the Portuguese word "barrocco", meaning an irregularly shaped pearl that was used in ornate jewelry. This small piece of extravagant finery typifies a period in which absolute monarchs reigned over Europe in all their finery, pomp, and grandeur. The explorations and inventions of the previous era had begun to pay off and the courts of Europe erupted in the splendor of squandered wealth. The court of Louis XIV at Versailles was an example of the incredible wealth evidenced by the ruling classes. Kings and princes rivaled each other to find and patronize the most famous artists, composers, and musicians. The highly embellished, ornate style of court music entered almost all forms of Baroque music.

With the supremacy of the nobility well established, the Catholic Church began to take second place in the affairs of the arts. The Church did hold sway over some Catholic composers who maintained the polyphonic tradition of Palestrina; while the Protestant Churches flourished in other parts of Europe and new forms of music were composed for their services. Religion was still an important part of life in the Baroque period, but it was often attended by conflict between Protestant and Catholic, and between Church and State. Many battles and wars were fought with religion as the excuse.

Science and exploration continued to play important roles in the affairs of Europe. Also, with great wealth flowing in from colonies, a new middle class emerged that began to grow in power and influence. The lavishness of the courts would soon give way to the oppressed majority.

Baroque Musical Style and Monody

The steps toward major/minor tonality had already been taken during the Renaissance. The use of leading tones, vertical awareness within the polyphonic style, the continued use of harmonies built on thirds and sixths, instrumental "chordal" accompaniments, and the bass functioning as a harmonic foundation all led up to the final steps out of modality. The rest of the development was a long process of developing a workable harmonic system through trial and error. This required most of the Baroque period to be accomplished.

113

The shift from a predominantly linear, melodic texture to the vertical, homophonic texture of Baroque music was given impetus shortly before the turn of the century (1600) by a group of Italian composers called the Camerata. They conceived the idea of bringing back Greek music and Classical ideals. Their conception of Greek music was based primarily on conjecture, since their major ideas were based on Greek writings and not the music itself. Their basic concept was to use music to heighten the emotional power of song texts. It was thought that the best way to do this was to simplify the accompaniment used to support the solo or vocal line, placing the emphasis on the melody. With the emphasis that had already begun to be placed on the bass part, it was a relatively small step to use the bass as a harmonic foundation for <u>chords</u>, built on thirds, to accompany the voice. This practice came partly from the lute and keyboard accompaniments of Renaissance secular songs in which the lower parts were often played as a chordal-type accompaniment, while the upper part was sung.

The simple chordal accompaniments that characterize this style initially do not relate specifically to the tension-release principles of major/minor tonality developed during this period. It took many years for these relationships between chords and keys to develop, but the first important step, conceiving the music harmonically rather than melodically, had taken place.

The chords of <u>monody</u> or solo, accompanied song were usually played on a keyboard instrument (harpsichord, clavichord, organ) or lute and a bass instrument. The bass part, called the <u>thorough bass</u>, or <u>basso continuo</u> (continuous bass) began to refer to the harmonic function of the bass part within a key; played on a low instrument with the chords filled in by the keyboard player. A <u>figured bass</u> was a shorthand notation for the basso continuo placed under the bass line to indicate to the keyboard player what chords he should play above a given bass note. The basso continuo part was played by two performers in Baroque music, a keyboard player and a bass instrument player.

The Baroque period also marked the shift to a steady metrical rhythm. Many of the basic rhythms of the Baroque were derived from dance forms, and many of the different types of instrumental music are written in dance rhythms. Even with the steady pulse now permeating most of the music, the effective sound of the musical

114

rhythm was one of a continuous flow. There was a continuous movement from the beginning of a section or movement toward the final cadence with no major interruptions by strong cadences. Some of the pieces maintained the freer rhythmic motion of earlier periods, particularly the improvisatory works.

One reason for the Baroque ideal of a continuous rhythmic flow was the conception that a piece of music or section should have one definite mood or <u>affection</u>. The Baroque composer achieved contrast by using contrasting movements, and thus contrasting moods, i.e. a fast movement follows a slow movement. As you listen to pieces from this period, you will be able to hear the effectiveness of the rhythmic flow coupled with the ideal of one affection. The drive of the music moves relentlessly toward its goal, and if you let it, it will sweep you into this forward motion.

Another aspect of Baroque music is the use of ornamentation. The Baroque composers expected the performers to add extra notes (turns, trills, and flourishes) in the performances. Eventually this practice of embellishing the music was written into the manuscripts by the composers. This use of ornamentation is descriptive of the gaudy, overly ornate styles of the courts.

Several important forms that developed in the Baroque period will be discussed later. Primarily, dance forms, repeated two-part forms (AABB), and improvisatory forms were popular.

The increasing refinement of instruments allowed the Baroque composer to be much more specific in assigning instruments to specific parts and in his use of dynamic markings. Dynamic markins now appeared in scores. The tendency was to have dynamics shift levels suddenly, <u>terraced dynamics</u>, rather than a gradual crescendo or decrescendo.

With the emphasis on harmony and harmonic progressions developing during the Baroque period it became important for the composers to be aware of the shifting from one key to another (modulations). When using true or just temperament (or true tuning based on the overtone series), the further away from the home key (tonic key) a composer modulated the more out of tune the music sounded. To alleviate this problem a new system of <u>equal temperament</u> gradually came into

115

practice in which the octave was divided into the twelve
equal half steps of our present system, not the unequal
steps of true temperament (see the overtone series, page
60). This tuning enabled composers to develop a relational harmonic system using all the keys of major/minor
tonality. It was most important for the keyboard instruments where the tuning could not be adjusted when modulating from key to key.

The transition from modality (modes) to tonality
was also gradual. During the Renaissance the use of the
raised leading tone in certain modes made those modes
sound very similar to major and minor scales. The transition to using major and minor scales exclusively took
many years and was primarily a preference in the sound
of these scales (half step and whole step patterns).

Baroque Vocal Music

The monodic style was adapted to a new form of
music found chiefly in the courts: opera. In Baroque
opera the grand arioso or aria, an elaborate solo song,
alternated with the simple declamation and accompaniment
of the recitative, where the vocal line imitated the
accents and patterns of speech. The opera was a grand,
elaborate production of mythological, heroic plots
which the nobility felt emulated their lives (a touch of
ego). The first opera is attributed to Peri in 1600--
"Euridice". The most important opera composers of the
period are Claudio Monteverdi (1567-1645) and later
George Frederick Handel (1685-1759). Originally centered in aristocratic courts, the opera under Handel's pen
reached out to the general public, the middle classes,
and became a popular form of entertainment.

However, Handel soon discovered that the middle
class was becoming increasingly dissatisfied with the
courtly orientation of opera and the idealistic plots,
consequently he began to write large vocal works with
Biblical texts, called oratorios. The oratorio is a
work for chorus, soloists, and orchestra, performed on
stage, but not meant to be acted or staged. The style
of music was virtually the same as in opera, with
recitatives alternating with arias, but the orientation
of the plot was much more acceptable to the general
public. Handel wrote many oratorios, the most famous of
which is the "Messiah": written in twelve days, it includes the wonderful "Hallelujah Chorus". (The entire
"Messiah" comprises over fifty separate numbers and
would take over three and a half fours to perform!) A

special form of the oratorio called the <u>Passion</u> was also popular. Its plot dealt specifically with the suffering and death of Christ, with the text taken from one of the Gospels.

Another group of vocal forms came from the music of the Lutheran Church. In the late Baroque the renowned master composer Johann Sebastian Bach (1685-1750) brought the development of Lutheran Church music to its greatest heights.

The most popular Lutheran vocal form was the <u>chorale</u>, a four part vocal work, in which the melody was often sung in unison by the congregation at the church services. These are homophonic (chordal) based melodies with Biblical or religious texts.

From the chorale a vast array of other vocal and instrumental works developed. The chorale cantatas of J.S.Bach were large pieces (approximately twenty to twenty-five minutes in length) written specifically for the Lutheran service and using chorale melodies as an inherent part of the composition. They could be solo cantatas (solo voice or several soloists); cantatas for chorus and orchestra; or cantatas for chorus, soloists, and orchestra. The texts were religious, usually associated with particular feast days, i.e. Bach's, "Christmas Cantata" is a series of six cantatas for various Christmas services.

Instrumental Music

For the first time in Western music history instrumental music began to rival the long dominance of vocal music. The forms of instrumental music began to develop separately from vocal music and dance, while retaining the characteristics of some of these forms.

A wide diversity of forms are seen in the works for keyboard instruments. Of particular importance are the "free forms". It was very popular for the performers at courts and churches to take themes from other works and improvise new works at the keyboard. This practice eventually developed into set pieces that were written down in the style of previous improvisations. Some of the improvisatory-based works are the fantasias, preludes, toccatas, inventions, and chorale preludes.

Often these free form movements would be coupled with a contrasting movement in a strict form, i.e. the toccata and fugue, or prelude and fugue. The <u>fugue</u> was a piece developed from the linear imitative polyphony of the Renaissance, but having a firm harmonic basis.) This use of contrasting movements gave the music of the Baroque period an interest it would not otherwise have had with the dominant ideal of one mood or affection per movement.

The keyboard instruments were also important for their consistent coupling in most instrumental works. The keyboard, generally the harpsichord, was an inherent part of the basso continuo which, in turn, was a part of almost all Baroque chamber and orchestral music.

In the early 1700's the first piano was invented; this instrument soon replaced the other keyboard instruments in many areas because of its capacity to be played at greatly diverse dynamic levels.

The pipe organ continued its reign as the chief instrument used in church and many thousands of important works for this instrument were written during this period. The avowed master of the organ was Johann Sebastian Bach, considered the greatest organ composer and perhaps the greatest composer in the history of Western music.

Many other important forms were derived from previous forms for both keyboard, solo instruments, and instrumental ensembles: <u>variation forms</u>, like the <u>passacaglia</u> and <u>chaconne</u> where the bass remained the same, either melodically or harmonically, and the treble varied; <u>dance</u> forms, including the Baroque <u>suite</u>--a collection of dance pieces (allemandes, courantes, sarabands, gigues, bourees, gavottes, and minuets to name a few)--specifically the <u>Sonata da Camera</u> or chamber sonata was a suite of dance forms usually composed for a small group of instruments; the <u>concerto grosso</u> forms (<u>concertato style</u>--contrasting a large group of instruments against a small group of instruments)--works for orchestra, the ripieno (full), and a contrasting smaller group of instruments, the concertino; the <u>Sonata da Chiesa</u> or church sonata--a piece usually of four movements, often slow, fast, slow, fast; and the <u>overture</u>, which originally preceded operas--the French style, slow-fast-slow sections, or Italian style, fast-slow-fast, which eventually developed into the symphony.

Many of these works varied considerably in the number and type of instruments for which they were written. The sonata was usually for solo instrument plus basso continuo or for a small group of instruments and basso continuo. A specific type of sonata was the trio sonata, so called because of its three parts (treble, treble, and continuo). However, this actually meant that the piece was played by four musicians: two treble instrument players (i.e. two violins), keyboard, and a bass instrument player (i.e. cello). The symphonic works, concerti grossi, overtures, sinfonias, et cetera, used a small orchestra--probably about twenty-five players, mostly strings, occasionally with a few woodwinds and/or brass, and sometimes groups of solo instruments (plus continuo).

The instruments continued to be refined and many of them basically reached the form that they are in today. The viols were replaced by the more resonant violin family (developed in the middle of the 16th century). The guitar replaced the lute, and many wind instruments were further refined (though valves on horns and trumpets did not appear until the 19th century). The clarinet developed around the mid-18th century. The percussion ensemble consisted mainly of drums.

The important growth of instrumental music can be traced to the rise of the middle class and its interest in musical training and performance. Instruments were more readily available than before, and the new standardizations helped make training in instrumental performance easier.

Bach and Handel

Another brief mention should be made of the two most important composers of the mature Baroque. Both J.S.Bach and G.F.Handel took the new idiom of major/ minor tonality and developed it into a workable system, while producing the most exquisite music. Those of you who have heard a live performance of the "Hallelujah Chorus" know the power and emotional strength of Handel's music. Bach also, perhaps in a more subtle, intellectual sense, can draw the listener into his music with its deep religious and emotional feeling.

Their styles differ greatly, Handel having written for the court and the public his whole life, and Bach for the Lutheran Church. However, each in his own way reached an incredible mastery over the new music of the Baroque. From here the music continued to develop and spoke a new language.

119

Rococo Period (1725-1775)

Around 1725 a new style emerged from the mature Baroque. Though it contained many elements of Baroque music it changed slowly into a new style that finally merged into Classicism. This Rococo period (from rocaille--shell) really overlaps the late Baroque and early Classical periods and it is a transitional period, where, in a sense, the elegance of the Baroque has a last say. The music is generally light, cheerful, even playful, delicate, and elegant. It is characterized by much ornamentation and a certain frivolity of style, for it was considered to be, to a certain extent, less serious music than that of the masters of the Baroque. Some of the Rococo composers are Telemann, Tartini, Vivaldi, C.P.E.Bach, J.C.Bach, and W.F.Bach (these last three were all sons of J.S.Bach and in their day were more famous than their father). Some characteristics, predecessors of Classicism, are the use of dynamic crescendos, and diminuendos, and dynamic accents, more cadences within a movement, and increased awareness of the harmonic language, or tension and release.

Chapter IV: Glossary

Baroque period: 1600-1750, period characterized by a grand, ornate style; the beginning of major/minor tonality and homophonic music

monody: solo accompanied song, simple chordal accompaniment

basso continuo, thorough bass: "continuous bass", part played by two performers, a keyboard player who filled in the harmony above the bass line, and a bass instrument player

figured bass: shorthand notation for keyboard performers to indicate what notes (chords) were to be played above the bass part of the basso continuo

terraced dynamics: levels of dynamics marked by sudden shifts and not gradual changes

affection: one mood, Baroque ideal of one mood or affection to a movement or section of a piece

ornamentation, embellishment: added notes, in Baroque practice the performer was expected to add notes to the score in performance

equal temperament: equal tuning; dividing the octave into twelve equal half steps

opera: large vocal work for stage production: used solos, chorus, and orchestra (later less use of chorus); in the Baroque period plots were mythologically and heroically based

aria: elaborate solo section of opera or oratorio

recitative: speech-like solo line accompanied by simple chordal harmony

George Frederick Handel: (1685-1759), famous opera and oratorio composer; also wrote many important instrumental works

oratorio: large vocal work similar to opera but not staged, used Biblical texts

Passion: oratorio on a Gospel text about the suffering and death of Christ

chorale: Lutheran four part hymn, chordal style, sung at service; usually melody sung in unison by congregation; Biblical or religious texts

cantata: (church cantata), large vocal work written for Lutheran service and feast days: solo, chamber, and choral canatas

improvisatory instrumental pieces: fantasias, preludes, toccatas, inventions, chorale preludes, et cetera

fugue: strict contrapuntal form, but with a firm harmonic basis

Johann Sebastian Bach: (1685-1750), great master of the Baroque; organist, composer of numerous works for Lutheran Church, including cantatas, Passions, organ works, instrumental works, et cetera

Baroque suite: collection of dance forms like the allemande, minuet, saraband, gigue, gavotte, courante, et cetera

variation forms: passacaglia and chaconne, and other forms where the method of composition is based on varying the melody, rhythm, harmony, et cetera

sonata da camera: chamber sonata--piece for small group of instruments; a suite of dance forms

sonata da chiesa: church sonata--piece of four movements, slow-fast-slow-fast

concerto grosso: piece for orchestra, ripieno, and contrasting smaller ensemble, concertino

concertato style: contrasting large group of instruments with a small group of instruments; see concerto grosso

overture: orchestral work used as prelude to opera; French overture, slow-fast-slow; Italian overture, fast-slow-fast, eventually developed into symphony form

Baroque sonata: piece for solo instrument(s). and basso continuo

trio sonata: piece for two treble instruments and basso continuo (four performers)

Rococo period: 1725-1775, transitional period from mature Baroque to early Classicism; elegant, ornate, "frivolous" style

Chapter V

Classical Period: 1750-1825

By 1750 the monarchies of Europe were facing the ire of the growing middle class and the oppressed lower class. The depletion by wars and the lavish extravagance of the dandies of Europe had taken too much toll on the people. This was the era of revolution: American, 1776; French, 1789; and the Industrial Revolution.

Within this political turmoil the arts continued to flourish. A new style emerged that banished the ornate style of the Baroque and Rococo and replaced it with order, structure, and clarity. The Classical artist and composer was very concerned with the control and discipline of his work. He emulated and idealized the Classical forms of ancient Rome and Greece. Striving for objectivity and tradition in art, he reached for the highest perfection in his art.

The music of the Classical period is very structured in form. Here we will explore again the forms discussed in the chapter on musical form in Section I of this text: sonata-allegro, variation, minuet and trio, and rondo forms (see pages 73-75). From single notes, short motives, and even accompanying passages, the Classical composer builds his music. The greatest of the Classical composers are those whose music has this extreme interior structure without it being imposed superficially on the music and its expressive purpose.

With their emphasis on order, the Classical composers took the initial understanding of the Baroque of harmony and built an elaborate system of tonal hierarchy centered on the relationship of the Tonic (I) and Dominant (V) chords (see Chapter V, Section I, on harmony). Each chord and each key became related in a very distinct way to every other chord and key. The true understanding of the tension and release relationships of major/minor chordal harmony were developed. The harmonic language in which chords and keys could be used grew rapidly during the Classical period. From simple relationships centered around the tonic and dominant harmonies in Haydn's early music the harmonic conception evolved to more complex relationships that moved further and further away from the original tonic/dominant reliance and reached finally to the use of frequent, extended modulations in Beethoven's music.

The texture of polyphony kept alive in Baroque fugues and inventions now virtually disappeared in favor of the chordal, dramatic emphasis of homophonic music. Though the great composers of Classicism used polyphony in their works to a certain extent, the harmonic idiom of melody and accompaniment prevails. With this we see quite a change in musical style. The one affection of Baroque music was replaced by the frequent cadencing (chord progressions coming to a point of rest, i.e. tension and release) and the multiple themes of Classicism. The contrast in Baroque music from one movement to another was now seen <u>within</u> the movement of a Classical work through the use of contrasting themes.

The subtleties of scoring are also affected by the <u>order</u> of the Classicists. The dynamic range increased throughout the period from pp to ff and simple accents to as many as six piano and forte markings (pppppp and ffffff) in Beethoven's music, as well as many accents, strong sforzandi, sudden shifts of dynamics, and increasing use of long crescendi and diminuendi. Tempo markings also became more illustrative of the composer's intent: they no longer simply wrote an allegro or andante, but allegro con spirito and andante con grazioso, <u>et</u> <u>cetera</u>. Changes in tempi are also included with the more frequent use of ritardandi, accelerandi, <u>et</u> <u>cetera</u>. (See page 32 for tempo markings)

The instruments of the Classical period had almost all reached their final basic forms. The Classical composers began to use more instruments in the orchestra: more winds, brass, and the timpani became important additions. The orchestras expanded in size to as many as fifty to sixty performers and the composers experimented more with instrumental combinations within the orchestra. Chamber music, string quartets, trios, <u>et</u> <u>cetera</u>, became an important form. The piano became THE accompanying instrument, replacing the harpsichord, and was also the primary solo instrument.

The Classical sonata form was used in a wide range of works: the <u>sonata</u>--for solo instrument or solo instrument and piano, three or four movements; the <u>symphony</u>--large orchestral work of three or four movements; and the <u>concerto</u>--a work for solo instrument and orchestra, usually three movements with the use of a <u>cadenza</u> in the first movement or in all three movements. (The cadenza is a brief passage where the soloist plays alone. This was originally improvised, but

today the cadenzas are played from composed manuscripts,
usually added to the original work. The cadenza was
used as a showcase for the performer's technical brilliance.)

Even in sonata form we see a continual expansion
during this period. Through the works of Haydn, Mozart,
and Beethoven (the three master Classical composers) the
form expands through additions of more thematic and
transitional material, greater extension in the development section, how the material in the exposition is used
throughout the piece, and more changes to the inner form
itself through more complex key relationships. The early
Haydn sonata-allegro movement might last five to ten
minutes; by late Mozart and Beethoven, it was likely
to be twice that long, or even longer.

We are going to take a closer look at the movement
structures of the Classical sonata. It would help to
review the discussion of these forms on pages 73-75 in
this text. Through the following examples you can get
a perspective of the organization in a Classical music
composition. Even if you do not read music you can probably follow the general outlines and ideas of the
examples.

Below are examples of the four movement types
(sonata-allegro, theme and variations, minuet and trio,
and rondo forms) discussed in the chapter on musical
form. This scoring shows only the breakdown of the
major themes and sections, in order to give you an idea•
of how the movements were put together. These movements
will be heard and discussed further in class.

Symphony #40 in g minor, K. 550   W.A.Mozart

First movement: Molto allegro

Sonata-Allegro Form

EXPOSITION: First theme in Tonic key, g minor

125

After this passage there is a repetition of this theme
slightly altered, and then a bridge passage which
modulates to the key of B-flat Major (The _relative_
major key to the key of g minor--meaning it has the
same number of flats.), a _closely_ _related_ key.

Bridge passage   modulates to B-flat major

The second theme enters in the key of B-flat Major.
Note the contrast of this theme from the first theme.

Second theme   in relative major, B-flat Major

The _codetta_ or closing section to the exposition contains passages of rapid eighth notes and several references back to the first theme:

Codetta passages:

Note rhythmic relationship to first theme here:

    The Exposition is _repeated_. In some recordings it
will not be repeated, due to the time factor, but it is
notated in the score by Mozart.)

DEVELOPMENT: development of themes

    Although the second theme is indicated in the
development in several places, this section is predominantly built on references to the first theme.

After an initial statement of the theme,

Mozart starts to break it into smaller and smaller segments:

and finally:

Extensive modulations in the development return the piece to the tonic for the:

RECAPITULATION: restatement of themes

> First theme is restated as in exposition in the tonic key of g minor.

> Bridge passage is slightly longer then in exposition.

> Second theme is now stated in the tonic key of g minor.

> The coda uses material from the first theme and cadences in the tonic key.

This first movement of Mozart's symphony is a classic example of sonata-allegro form (first movement form). As mentioned in the chapter on form this basic structure can be varied in different ways. The essential ingredients are movement away from the tonic key (tension, [here, the modulation to the relative major key]) and the return to the tonic (release), and repetition (exposition, recapitulation) and contrast (between first and second theme, and the development section--variation of themes and modulations).

The second type of movement we will look at closely is the theme and variations, slow movement form.

This is from a Haydn string quartet.

String Quartet in B-flat Major, Op. 50 No.1

F.J.Haydn

Second movement: Adagio non lento

Theme:

The whole theme comprises two sections of six measures each. The accompaniment in the second violin and viola is similar to the cello.

Variation I:

> second violin on theme, first violin on a new accompaniment figure, viola and cello same as before:

The variation is also in two sections, each of six measures.

Variation II:

> first violin back on theme one octave higher, second violin and viola on new accompaniment figures:

Variation III:

The melody continues in the first violin and there is now a thirty-second note accompaniment in the cello part.

Variation IV: Closing Section

Melody itself is varied with ornamentation of sixteenth and thirty-second notes.

The important aspect of this form is its extreme symmetry, i.e. each section six measures times two. Also important is the inherent concept of repetition and contrast in the theme and variations form itself. Here the variations consist of changes in accompaniment, the instrument on the melody, the range of the melody, and embellishment of the melody.

The minuet and trio is perhaps the strictest form of the four discussed here. The following, from a Haydn symphony, is typical of the idiom.

Symphony in D Major, "London"   F.J.Haydn

Third movement: Allegro

Minuet: First section theme,

In the minuet the first section is not repeated; second section is repeated. Often in this form both sections of the minuet will be repeated.

Trio: Theme,

The two sections of the trio are each repeated. Note
the contrast in the theme of the minuet (separate,
staccato notes) to the theme of the trio (long and
sustained).

Minuet da capo: There is a return to the minuet and it
is played without repeats the second time through. The
minuet and trio form is always in triple meter, here
3/4.

        The last form we will look at is the rondo form,
an alternating form. The following is from a Beethoven
sonata for violin and piano. The form is an A B A C A
B A form.

Sonata for Violin and Piano in F Major, Op. 24

                                    L. van Beethoven

        Fourth movement: Rondo--Allegro ma non troppo

First theme:

A section, stated in piano and then violin.

Second theme: three different ideas presented,

Sustained eighths followed by trills,

then a quarter and sixteenth note figure,

and finally a triplet passage with a return to the trills, B section.

Return of A section in piano, then violin, slightly altered, i.e. A'.

Third theme:

C section, alternates a sustained melody in piano (then violin) with triplets in violin (then in piano).

A section returns and is again slightly varied, A''.

B section returns in a different key, B'.

A section returns for the final time with ornamentation added to violin part, A'''.

There is also a short closing section with elements of the B and C theme triplets predominating.

The overall concept of musical form is relatively simple, mentioned frequently in this text, repetition and contrast, tension and release. The Classicists were perhaps more aware of the abstract structure of form than composers from other periods, but in the final analysis the expressive content derived from whatever system is used is the most important aspect of the

131

music. If you are aware of this conception of musical form, you can apply your knowledge to listening experiences and begin to apprehend some of the deeper significances of classical music.

Three Major Classical Composers

A brief look at the major Clasical composers will help show the extent of their production of instrumental works. Franz Joseph Haydn (1732-1809) was the most prolific Classical composer of the three we will study, and the only composer of them to remain under court patronage almost his entire life. He produced 104 symphonies, 83 string quartets, numerous other chamber and orchestral works, many solo sonatas for piano and for piano with other instruments, and various concerti. His music developed continually through his entire life as he experimented with Classical harmony and form.

Wolfgang Amadeus Mozart (1751-1791) lived a difficult life without the security of patronage and he died a pauper. His output is remarkable, considering his short life and constant worry over his financial situation. He wrote 41 symphonies, numerous string quartets and other chamber works, many fine concerti for piano, violin, horn, flute, and other instruments, sonatas, and other symphonic works. His music is wonderfully lyrical with melodies reminiscent of his operas.

The master of the late Classical period and forerunner of the Romantic period is Ludwig van Beethoven (1770-1827). Beethoven had to work very hard to produce the music that churned within him. His life and work were made even more difficult by his increasing deafness, which became complete in his later life. His music is a culmination of Classical idioms and late in life a reaching out toward the emotionality and the musical complexities of Romanticism. He wrote 9 symphonies, 18 string quartets, other chamber works, overtures, numerous sonatas, including 32 piano sonatas and a variety of concerti.

Vocal Music

The vocal music of the Classical period, both religious and secular does not compare with the output of instrumental works of the period. However, each of the Classical masters produced fine works in this idiom.

The Masses (12) of Haydn and his two oratorios

("The Creation" and "The Seasons") are considered his most important vocal works. His twenty operas are considered lesser works and are rarely performed today.

Mozart was the greatest opera composer of the Classical period. His operas are considered to be some of the finest ever written. The Italian and German people loved opera and it was a popular form throughout the Classical period. Mozart's lyrical operatic style permeates all of his instrumental works. He also wrote several Masses that are often performed today. (The Classical Mass was not considered to be a <u>functional</u> religious work. It was written to be performed, not for use in church services.) Mozart's Requiem, written in his last months of life and incomplete at his death, is one of his most beautiful works. It was completed by one of his students from Mozart's sketches.

Beethoven's most famous choral work is the finale (last movement) of his ninth symphony. He also wrote one opera, "Fidelio", still considered an important work, several Masses, and some solo songs. But he was primarily an instrumental composer and his vocal works are considered very difficult to sing.

The Classical emphasis on instrumental music shows the increased participation in music by the middle class. The piano had become the instrument which replaced the harpsichord, and it became an important solo and chamber instrument. Instruments and music, through publishing, printing, and standardization, became more available to the general public. The demise of the practice of patronage had forced composers (i.e. Mozart and Beethoven) to sell their works to publishers and to write for the public's taste. A new era was blossoming where the Church and State no longer controlled and influenced the artistic output.

Chapter V: Glossary

Classical period: 1750-1825, very ordered and structured
style; use of "absolute" forms: sonata-allegro, minuet
and trio, theme and variations, rondo, et cetera

large Classical forms:

> sonata: work for piano, or solo instrument and
> piano in three or four movements

> chamber music: quartets, trios, et cetera, usually
> in three or four movements

> symphony: work for full orchestra, in three
> or four movements

> concerto: work for solo instrument and orchestra,
> usually in three movements with cadenzas

cadenza: section in a concerto where the performer plays
alone, originally improvised on themes from the concerto, used as a showcase for performer's technical
brilliance

Classical composers:

> F.J.Haydn 1732-1809

> W.A.Mozart 1756-1791

> L. van Beethoven 1770-1827

Chapter VI

The Romantic Period: 1825-1900

Ah! The Romantic spirit. The effusive artistic
poetry that flowed from the pen of the Romantic soul.
Inspiration, spontaneity, the richness of emotions
poured forth as a complete reversal of the ordered soul
of the Classicists. The Romantic artist gave rein to
his emotions, inspired by the senses, the mysterious
and exotic, nature, passion, dreams. His ultimate per-
sonification was the hero striving always for his ideals
and dreams, but failing, and eventually receiving salvation from his religious convictions. The heart is
what should guide you, not order and form, Love!
Tommorrow is but a dream!

Musically, the Romantic composer burst the bonds
set by Classicism. Already Beethoven's later works had
begun to strain under the chains of the Classical forms
and harmony; the Romantics virtually ignore them in
their ultimate search for expression. The Romantics
were interested in the fusion of the arts--combining
literature, drama, dance, and music into one large form.
In some of the great operas of the period this ideal
is amazingly achieved.

The growth of music was seen in many areas.
Beethoven's orchestra of 50-60 players expanded to the
huge proportions of the late Romantic composers
(Richard Strauss, Gustav Mahler, et cetera) where well
over a hundred instrumentalists might be used, and in
numerous works a full chorus and soloists are added to
the symphony. New instruments were added to the orchestra: of particular interest to the Romantic were such
"exotic" instruments as chimes, bells, triangles,
cymbals, et cetera. The wind and brass sections expanded
in size, and a much wider range of percussion was used.
The technique of performance reached incredibly demanding heights. The pianist/composer Franz Liszt took
piano technique to demonic limits and a violinist/
composer, Niccolo Paganini did the same for the violin.

The Romantic composers took old forms of Classicism
and used them in a very free style and also developed
new forms to fit their ideal of freedom of expression.
More complex harmonic relationships developed until, by
the end of the period, with the late Romantic composers
like Wagner, Mahler, and Mussorgsky, the "functional"
harmonic relationships of Classicism had almost

completely disappeared. In Romantic music tension was created through the use of complex chord progressions and modulations that only resolved (released) with the eventual return to a key center, rather than through the dominant/tonic relationship of Classicism. A piece by a Romantic composer can take you along for twenty minutes before you ever get the "relief" of a return to the tonic. Major/minor tonality was already on the way out in classical music. Its reign was very brief in the history of Western music--barely two hundred years.

The formal structure of the music of the Romantics was essentially free. Some of the more conservative Romantic composers (Brahms, Mendelssohn, Bruckner, Schubert) followed the general outlines of Classical forms fairly closely, but the more radical Romantics (Berlioz, Richard Strauss, Wagner), and to a certain extent all Romantic composers developed free-form compositions.

The symphony form expanded in length and in number of movements: Mahler's symphonies can last almost two hours and have four, five, or six movements. Sonatas, chamber music, concerti, and other Classical pieces were all written by the Romantics but the formal structure was very loose and sometimes non-existent in the sense of the Classical order. The true Romantic form is seen in the development of the short piece. The piano was particularly adapted to short compositions of Romantic nature: fantasias, mazurkas, etudes, waltzes, preludes, impromptus. These were short, free-form compositions ranging from a minute or longer in length.

The Romantic spirit was particularly adaptable to a form of music that became known as program music. This meant that a "program" or description of the piece would be used to help describe the composer's ideas or conceptions in relationship to the work. Descriptive titles on short works, such as Saint-Saens', "The Swan", were considered programmatic. A popular form of program music was the tone poem or symphonic poem. This is an orchestral piece, usually in one long movement, such as Liszt's "Les Preludes", R. Strauss's, "Thus Spake Zarathustra" or "Til Eulenspiegel's Merry Pranks". (A story about a trickster and his pranks, who finally gets hanged for his misdeeds--one can hear the march to the gallows and the trapdoor fall in the final moments of the work.) Many other works of this period are also programmatic: symphonies, i.e. Mendelssohn's "Spring" symphony, sonatas, chamber works, et cetera. The programs could be specific stories like "Til Eulenspiegel", or general conceptions, like "Spring", or even ideals, "A Hero's Life", by R. Strauss. The story or idea was substituted for more traditional means of organization.

In vocal music a new form emerged as an ideal form of expression for the Romantic emotion. The art song developed as a work for solo voice and piano. In the works of Franz Schubert (the master of this idiom) the piano and voice achieved a remarkable balance. Thus two popular instruments of the period were welded into a rich, expressive medium. The songs are of love, nature, death, and idealism. They are either strophic or through-composed and are sometimes combined into song cycles that tell a story (Schubert's "Die Winterreise" is an excellent example. The twenty-four songs of the cycle tell a story about a lover who is rejected by his beloved, and who then wanders about in the winter landscape.) In listening to the art song it is important to pay close attention to the piano part, as it often "paints" the story of the text in conjunction with the vocal line. Other important composers of the art song are Hugo Wolf, Robert Schumann, Johannes Brahms, and Richard Strauss.

Larger forms of vocal music remained in the repetoire of the composers. Requiems (Masses for the Dead), Masses, symphonies with chorus, other large vocal works and forms of religious music were written. Almost all the religious works were "non-functional", that is, meant to be performed in concert, rather than used in a church service.

Opera remained a favorite medium. The great early Romantic Italian opera composers, Bellini, Donizetti, Rossini, started where Mozart left off in developing the "bel canto" (""beautiful singing", elaborate") style. This was a light virtuoso singing style that required tremendous range and technical ability.

Later in the period opera achieved a grander, dramatic, almost heavier quality (Grand Opera), including ballet, crowd scenes, large choruses and ensembles with massive, elaborate sets. The foremost composers were Guiseppe Verdi, Giacomo Puccini, Charles Gounod, and Georges Bizet. The period culminated in the works of the German master Richard Wagner. He took the total artistic medium and created heroic operas combining dance, voice, drama, and literature (the libretto, which is the story and words or lines of the opera) into the Romantic ideal of a complete artistic expression.

The piano was THE instrument of the Romantic. Besides a very large output of small lyrical pieces, the composers wrote for the piano in many forms: sonatas, concerti, larger programmatic works, i.e. Mussorgsky's, "Pictures at an Exhibition", and works for two pianos or also for two pianists at one piano (piano four hands). Since the piano was readily available to the general public, it was fairly easy to learn to play at least simple tunes if one struck the right keys and one did not have the intonation problems of other instruments.

Chamber music continued to be an important idiom. The piano played a primary role in combinations with string instruments: piano quartet, piano trio, <u>et cetera</u>, and wind chamber music was also important.

More than that of any other period the music of the Romantic period can be defined by national boundaries. <u>Nationalism</u> in music emphasizes particular elements of a country's culture, the local "color". In some forms, like purely instrumental music, the distinction is not always so obvious, but other forms, opera and song being good examples, the language used and its special inflections, can greatly affect the nuances of the music. Thus a French song written during the Romantic period was very different from a German song; and French opera was substantially different from German or Italian opera. But even more to the point, true nationalism developed from the use of folk idioms of a country's heritage, or the use of national subjects for program music, opera, song, <u>et cetera</u>. Some composers collected elements of folk music from various countries and incorporated the idioms into their own musical styles: Liszt's, "Hungarian Dances", Dvorak's, "New World Symphony" (referring to America, which he visited). Many composers used their own national idioms, of course.

It would be difficult to talk in any detail about the many fine composers of the Romantic period and their works in this brief overview of music history, but it would also be remiss not to mention very briefly some of the major composers and part of their output. Listed on the next two pages are some of the major composers of the period.

Romantic composers:

Hector Berlioz: 1803-1869, French: tone poems, opera

Johannes Brahms: 1824-1896, German: piano music, songs,
    symphonies, major choral works, concerti, chamber
    music

Anton Bruckner: 1824-1896, Austrian: religious composer,
    symphonies, major choral works

Frederick Chopin: 1810-1849, Polish: piano music

Antonin Dvorak: 1841-1904, Bohemian (Czech): symphonies,
    chamber music

Cesar Franck: 1822-1890, French: symphonies, chamber
    music

Edvard Grieg: 1843-1907, Norwegian: tone poems, piano
    music, chamber music

Franz Liszt: 1811-1886, Austrian/Hungarian: virtuoso
    pianist, piano music, symphonies, tone poems,
    major choral works

Gustav Mahler: 1860-1911, Austrian: large scale sym-
    phonies, vocal music

Felix Mendelssohn: 1809-1847, German: symphonies,
    chamber music, piano music, oratorios, choral
    works

Niccolo Paganini: 1782-1840, Italian: virtuoso violinist,
    violin music

Franz Schubert: 1797-1828, Viennese: art songs, sym-
    phonies, Masses, chamber works, piano music

Robert Schumann: 1810-1856, German: piano music, art
    songs, symphonies, chamber music

Jean Sibelius: 1865-1957, Finnish: symphonies, tone
    poems

Johann Strauss the Younger: 1825-1899, Viennese: the
    waltz king

Richard Strauss: 1864-1949, German: tone poems, opera,
    songs

Peter Ilyich Tchaikovsky: 1840-1893, Russian: ballets,
    symphonies, opera, songs

Hugo Wolf: 1860-1903, German: art songs

Russian composers:

    Alexander Borodin: 1833-1887

    Modest Mussorgsky: 1839-1881

    Rimsky-Korsakov: 1844-1908

American composers:

    Edward MacDowell: 1861-1908

    John Phillip Sousa: 1854-1932

Opera composers:

    Vincenzo Bellini: 1801-1835, Italian

    Georges Bizet: 1838-1875, French

    Gaetano Donizetti: 1797-1848, Italian

    Charles Gounod: 1818-1893, French

    Giacomo Puccini: 1858-1924, Italian

    Gioacchino Rossini: 1792-1868, Italian

    Camille Saint-Saens: 1835-1921, French

    Guiseppe Verdi: 1813-1901, Italian

    Richard Wagner: 1813-1883, German

    You may have noticed the lack of American composers
in the history of Western music to this point. Except
for Edward MacDowell, piano composer, and John Phillip
Sousa, the march king, both composers of the Romantic
era, American music was centered around the importation
of European scores and musicians. American classical
music was only in its infancy and it is not until the
modern era that American composers come out of the
shadow of European dominance. Of course there were

many rich folk and jazz idioms developing in the United States during this time and they have a profound influence on twentieth century music.

Chapter VI: Glossary

Romantic period: 1825-1900, emphasis in the arts on emotion, passion, spontaneity

short lyric piano works: short, free-form piano pieces popular during the Romantic period--fantasias, mazurkas, etudes, waltzes, preludes, impromptus, et cetera

tone poem, symphonic poem: orchestral free-form work, program music, usually one long movement

art song: piece for solo voice and piano, instruments are ideally balanced, strophic or through-composed, poem set to music, usually of high literary quality

song cycle: collection of art songs that tells a story

Requiem: Mass for the dead

libretto: story of an opera, the words or lines

Grand Opera: generally associated with French opera of the Romantic period, but typically using large choruses, ensembles, crowd scenes, ballet, and massive elaborate sets

bel canto: "beautiful singing"; singing style of early Romantic opera from Mozart's heritage; light, high, technically very demanding music

nationalism: use of folk idioms and local "color" in a composition

Chapter VII

Modern Era: 1900-present

The modern era of music can best be described as
a period of continuous expansion and experimentation.
The Romantics had taken the major/minor tonal system to
its limits and newer forms of harmony were being search-
ed out. New instruments were constantly being added to
the standard groupings and old instruments began to be
used in new ways. In comparison to previous periods one
could say that in modern classical music, "almost anything goes".

Impressionism: 1890-1925 (approximate)

The first break with the effusive spirit of the
Romantics came in Paris at the turn of the century.
This new movement, called Impressionism, is characterized by the artist'a attempt to capture <u>impressions</u> of
things rather than a realistic portrayal, or its obvious characteristics. The music of the Impressionists
is still somewhat programmatic, with descriptive titles
for many of the works, i.e. Debussy's, "La Mer" (The
Sea). However, the music is of a very different mood
and texture from the typically Romantic work. Impressionists tend to use very large orchestras with many
exotic instruments and a full range of winds, brass,
and percussion, but the texture overall is light and
transparent. They rarely use the entire power of the
large ensemble, whereas the Romantics relished the
overwhelming sound of its full potential. Impressionistic music is often described in such terms as "cloudy",
"ethereal", and "with sensuous tone colors". The composers strive to create in their music the atmosphere
and mood of their subject.

The music itself is created from a variety of old
and new techniques. The Impressionists return to the
distant past and use the Medieval modes as a basis for
some of their works. New scales are also used: the
pentatonic scale, a scale of five notes in the octave;
many folk melodies are based on pentatonic scales. And
they also used the whole tone scale with six notes in
an octave, each note a whole step apart. Both these
scales are tonal in the sense that they have a tonal
center--the first note of the scale.

Pentatonic Scale   Whole tone Scale

Traditional major/minor tonality, in a widely expanded harmonic language, uses blocks of chords that
shift in parallel motion from chord to chord and key
to key without any emphasis on resolutions or strong
cadences. New chords are also introduced in the expanded
harmony of Impressionism (ninth chords, eleventh chords,
and thirteenth chords), creating new sounds.

parallel chords ninth chord eleventh thirteenth

Dissonance thus becomes an entity in itself without
any strong relationship to consonance, except the final
return to the tonal center.

The formal aspects of Impressionism are similar to
those of Romanticism. Impressionists are fond of short
pieces, particularly those written for piano. Tone
poems, relaxed Classical forms, and standard ensemble
forms are all used effectively. Transparency of texture
is achieved by subtle use of dynamic shadings and increasing use of <u>mutes</u> (a mute is a device placed on
or in an instrument to dampen the sound) on instruments.

The leaders of the Impressionistic movement, which
was centered in Paris, France, were Claude Debussy
(1862-1918) and Maurice Ravel (1875-1937). Other composers who were influenced by this style included:
Ralph Vaughan Williams, English; Frederick Delius, English; Manuel De Falla, Spanish; and Ottorino Respighi,
Italian.

Expressionism

Another style, which emerged during the second
decade of the 1900's in Vienna, was the complete
antithesis of Impressionism. <u>Expressionism</u> was an
attempt to portray the inner experience of man in music

and art. The Expressionist was interested in the psychology of experience, dream worlds, the supernatural, and the weird. This was a movement of abstraction--distorted shape in musical language and tone color.

The music of Expressionism is difficult for the average untrained ear to listen to, and even for some trained ones. It is sometimes described as "good music for horror films". The Expressionist experimented with new combinations of sounds that finally led to a complete dissolution of the major/minor tonal system. A form of composition emerged called serialism, serial music, or Twelve-tone techniques.

Serial music is a technique where the composer takes a specified number of notes (in twelve-tone music all twelve notes of the octave) and arranges them into a series. This "scale" or series is then used as the basis for the entire composition. The techniques of serial music are the same basic techniques used in imitative counterpoint: augmentation, diminution, retrograde, inversion. Also! the serial composer must follow the exact order of his set series of notes, using each note in order before he returns to use the series again. This might sound as though it would become incredibly boring, with the series continually being stated in one order, but the composer could also use the notes from the series vertically (which counts as using them in order) to produce a variety of unusual harmonies.

Twelve-tone series, or tone row

Serial music is the first real example of what became known as atonality--having no tonal center. With each note of a series theoretically remaining equal (no note having more emphasis, like a tonic or dominant), there is no tonal center to return to. Music had reached a new stepping stone in harmonic language. The major exponents of Expressionism were: Arnold Schoenberg (1874-1951), and his students, Alban Berg (1885-1935) and Anton Webern (1883-1947).

New Conceptions in Music

The easiest way to describe the great changes that have taken place in Twentieth century music is to review some of the basic aspects of music on an individual basis. Melody, harmony, rhythm, texture, sonority all expand to new horizons.

Melody

Melody in modern music takes on a more instrumental than vocal shape. That is, the music of earlier periods was lyrical, had a narrow range, mostly stepwise motion; i.e. it was relatively easy to sing. Modern melody is vastly extended in range, typically has wide dissonant leaps, and is very difficult to sing unless one has perfect pitch. The melodies require much greater concentration on the part of the listener. To follow them he must listen intellectually, not <u>just</u> emotionally. It is difficult to sit back and enjoy the majority of modern "tunes". One reason we do not leave the auditorium humming the tunes from a modern composition we have heard is because the contemporary composer also avoids repetition of his melodies, and the melodies are also often long and very drawn out. A good descriptive word for many modern melodies is "angular".

Harmony

As we have seen with Impressionism (ninth, eleventh, thirteenth chords; whole tone and pentatonic scales; and Medieval modes) and Expressionism (serial techniques) the harmony of modern music took off in many directions. Other practices also developed: <u>poly-harmony</u>/<u>poly-tonality</u>--use of two or more tonal centers at the same time (C major and F major for instance); <u>cluster chords</u>--chords built from intervals of a second (press the palm of your hand down on the piano keyboard!); construction of new scales and the use of oriental scales; use of <u>micro-tones</u>--intervals smaller than a half step; and virtually any combination that composers can think up.

Quartal harmony   Cluster chord   Polychord

Rhythm

The modern era expands the use of rhythm in two contrasting directions: toward total freedom or toward absolute control. Absolute control is possible with the advent of the precision of computers and electronic instruments. The move toward freedom is seen in the attempt to avoid the metrical "strangulation" of the barline. Syncopation (off-beats, from jazz idioms); unusual meters-- 13/16, 18/8, et cetera; poly-meter-- several meters going on at the same time (4/4 in one part, 6/8 in another); changing meters; avoidance of metrical accents; and primitive rhythms, all added up to variety in the composers' rhythmic language. The final aspect of rhythmic freedom is when the composer leaves the length of notes to be played up to the discretion of the performer, making each performance different. On the other side of absolute rhythmic control, composers begin to serialize rhythms in the same sense as the melodic serial techniques--absolute adherence to a set pattern.

Texture and Sonority

The major trend in texture and sonority in modern music is toward a lightening of the overall sound. Even with the large orchestral forces available, the modern composer uses the massive sound only occasionally, preferring to develop the subtlety and finesse of combinations of individual instruments. Solos are used with great frequency within the large orchestral works and subtle changes of color are favored. Polyphony returns to common usage, adding linear beauty to the previously predominant homophonic idioms of the Classicists and Romantics. The contemporary composers return once more to the Classical ideals of clarity and order.

Form

The modern composer looks back to the symmetry of Classical structure and form on the one hand, and toward total freedom on the other. He likes to avoid repetition, but the "absolute" forms of Classicism appeal to his sense of control. Other composers strive toward freedom, using free form to the extent of leaving the structure of the final performance up to the performers themselves: One score reads, "Continue playing this section until everyone else quits."--somewhat indefinite.

A Word about Listening to Twentieth Century Music

Many people complain, and in a few cases justly, that modern music is too intellectual. There are two answers to that accusation: yes, it is intellectually based, more perhaps than in other periods, but then the Romantics were on the other side of the fence, some would say overly emotional. A person's preference should decide the issue. The other answer is that there certainly is emotion in most Twentieth century music. It may not always be the emotion you want to feel, and you must make an effort to be aware of the composer's intent. Sometimes the contemporary composer hits us where it hurts the most, with <u>feelings</u> of fear, hate, horror, disgust, <u>et</u> <u>cetera</u>, in his music. Understanding may not breed appreciation, but at least respect, and perhaps a knowledge that you had not acquired before. Above all modern music is a realm to be explored. There ARE joys, sorrows, laughs, tears to discover in the music, but YOU must make the effort to explore this continually expanding art form.

Other Trends

New techniques and styles are constantly being explored by contemporary composers. It is worth a brief look at some of the past and current trends in modern musical practice.

<u>Neo-Classicism</u>: return to order and structure of Classical music, simple, clarity in music--Igor Stravinsky, Bela Bartok representative composers

<u>Primitivism</u>: use of African, South American, <u>et</u> <u>cetera</u>, rhythms; emphasis on percussive drive in the music--Stravinsky

<u>Gebrauchsmusik</u>: Work-a-day music; music for the people, easy listening, educational, music that could be used by the public--Paul Hindemith

<u>Jazz</u>: use in classical music--George Gershwin, Darius Milhaud

<u>Aleatoric</u> <u>music</u>: chance music, music that is composed by chance, i.e. a composer might write a piece based on a melody associated with the numbers in his girl friend's phone number

<u>Pointilism</u>: "Points of sound"; instruments play short

148

"dots" of sound; music tends to have more silence than sound

Electronic music: Use of electronic devices to produce music: synthesizers, computers, tape recorders, manufactured sounds, syne (pure) tones--Karlheinz Stockhausen

Soviet music: music written by Russian composers in Russia, somewhat under the "guidance" of the Soviet government--Dmitri Shostakovich, Sergei Prokofiev

Russian music: music written by Russian composers who left Russia--Igor Stravinsky

Total Serialization: controlling all the elements of music by serialization techniques, i.e. melody, harmony, tone color, rhythm, and form--Olivier Messiaen

Musique concrete: recorded sounds used in compositions, i.e. bird calls, train whistle, et cetera--Pierre Henry, Olivier Messiaen

American Composers

During the modern era American composers have come into their own. Many fine composers have produced an exceptional volume of work, that is considered important music today. How much of this will survive the centuries it is impossible to say for the composers we laud today may be forgotten in the future. American composers have expressed themselves in many ways, using old techniques and also new experimental forms; of particular interest is the folk and jazz heritage of our country used by some of these composers in their work. Listed below are a few of the well-known American composers:

Milton Babbitt (1916-)

John Cage (1912-)

Elliott Carter (1929-)

Aaron Copland (1900-)

Henry Cowell (1897-1965)

George Crumb (1929-)

George Gershwin (1898-1937)

Howard Hanson (1896-1981)

Roy Harris (1898-)

Charles Ives (1874-1954), an insurance salesman, and one of the foremost innovators in music history

Walter Piston (1894-1976)

Carl Ruggles (1876-1971)

Roger Sessions (1894-1976)

The world of contemporary music is a strange and wonderful world to explore. It is impossible to give credit to all the well-known European and American composers in such a short space. It is a new world and new worlds are meant to be explored.

Chapter VII: Glossary

Modern music: 1900-present, "Twentieth century music", "contemporary music", music represented by continued expansion and experimentation

Impressionism: attempt to give "impression" of world, things, et cetera; "cloudy", transparent texture; use of Medieval modes, whole tone and pentatonic scales, ninth, eleventh, and thirteenth chords

Expressionism: "expressing" inner experience, dream-worlds, supernatural; use of twelve-tone, serial techniques

pentatonic scale: five note scale, i.e. C D F G A (C)

whole tone scale: six note scale within the octave; each note a whole step apart, i.e. C D E F# G# A# (C)

serial techniques, twelve-tone music: serialism, arranging notes in series that is then used as a basis for a composition

20th century melody: angular, wide leaps, large range, long melodies poly-harmony/poly-tonality: use of two or more tonal centers at one time

polychords: superimposing different chords

quartal harmony: chords built on the interval of a fourth

cluster chords: chords built on interval of a second

micro-tones: intervals smaller than a half step

20th century rhythm: unusual meters, poly-meters, changing meters, primitive rhythms, syncopation and jazz rhythms, absolute versus free rhythm

20th century texture and sonority: lightening of over-all sound, experimentation with new instruments, use of old instruments in new ways

20th century form: return to Classical structure and order, OR striving toward total freedom

Neo-Classicism: return to order and structure of Classical music, simple, clear music

Primitivism: use of African and other primitive rhythms, emphasis on percussive drive

Gebrauchsmusik: music for the people

Aleatoric music: chance music

Pointillism: points, dots of sound; music tends to have more silence than sound

Soviet music: music written by composers in Russia under the eye of the Soviet government

Russian music: music written by composers who left Russia

Total Serialization: controlling all the elements of music by serialization techniques

Musique concrete: tape recorded sounds used in compositions

History of Western Music: Progressive Chart

Greek Music	Medieval Period	Renaissance
600BC-300BC	400AD-1450	1450-1600

900AD

monophonic------------------------Early Polyphony---------Imitative Polyphony-----

Greek-----/ /Medieval modes--
modes

Baroque Period	Classical Period	Romantic Period	Modern Period
1600-1750	1750-1825	1825-1900	1900-present

Homophonic Music--

Major/Minor Tonality-------------------------------------contemporary tonality
                                                         and atonality

Bibliographical Acknowledgements

The author acknowledges an appreciation and debt to the following works for long and continued contact through study and use in the classroom.

Apel, Willi, Harvard Dictionary of Music, Cambridge, Massachusetts: Harvard University Press, 1968.

Einstein, Alfred, Music in the Romantic Era, New York: W.W. Norton & Company, Inc., 1947.

Grout, Donald Jay, A History of Western Music, 3rd ed., New York: W.W.Norton & Company, 1980.

Rosen, Charles, The Classical Style, New York: W.W. Norton & Company, 1972.

The following works were consulted for general format and style as a guide to writing this text. The author has endeavored to present all material in a completely original fashion.

Borroff, Edith and Irvin, Marjory, Music in Perspective, New York: Harcourt Brace Jovanovich, Inc., 1976.

Daniels, Arthur and Wagner, Lavern (ed), Listening to Music, New York: Holt, Rinehart and Winston, 1975

Hickock, Robert, Exploring Music, Reading, Massachusetts: Addison-Wesley Pub. Co., 1979.

Hoffer, Charles, The Understanding of Music, 3rd ed., Belmont, California: Wadsworth Pub. Co., Inc., 1976.

Kerman, Joseph, Listen, New York: Worth Publishers, Inc., 1980

Machlis, Joseph, The Enjoyment of Music, 4th ed., New York: W.W.Norton & Company. Inc., 1977.

Politoske, Daniel T., Music, Englewood Cliffs, New Jersey: Prentice-Hall, Inc., 1979.

Sacher, Jack and Eversole, James, The Art of Sound: An Introduction to Music, 2nd. ed., Englewood Cliffs, New Jersey: Prentice-Hall, Inc., 1977.

Schindler, Allan, <u>Listening to Music</u>, New York: Holt,
Rinehart and Winston, 1980.

Wingell, Richard, <u>Experiencing Music</u>, Sherman Oaks,
California: Aldref Publishing Co., Inc., 1981.